To Jacob

Thankyou and i
hope you really
enjoy this book!!

About the Author

The author is a normal working lad from Teesside, who due to illness found himself off sick. Attempting to keep his mind active, Johnalan decided to write his niece and nephews a story. This is part one of the trilogy and he hopes readers will enjoy it.

Dedication

I would like to thank my friends and family for their participation in this book and the ones to come. THANK YOU.

Johnalan Wright

DISCO DANBY

AUSTIN MACAULEY
PUBLISHERS LTD.

A CIP catalogue record for this title is available from the British Library.

ISBN 978 1 78455 192 6

www.austinmacauley.com

First Published (2015)
Austin Macauley Publishers Ltd.
25 Canada Square
Canary Wharf
London
E14 5LB

Printed and bound in Great Britain

Disco Danby Character Index

Neutrals:

Zeus – Greek Father of the Gods, Sky God
Hades – Greek God of the Underworld Aput, Egyptian messenger
   god
Purusha – Hindu Mystic Dwarf God
Herophilus's – Chemist to the Gods and Ruler of the Realm of
   Learning
Cheeves – Winged Skeletons of Lost Gods
Poseidon – Greek God of the Sea
Odin – Norse Father God

Of the same thought as Mother Nature:

Mother Nature – Pagan Goddess, Mother of the Earth
Wickons – Mother Nature's Subjects
Schmee – Friends of Mother Nature and the Wickons. Capable of
   Morphing
Cernunnos – Celtic God of the Wild Hunt, Fertility and Masculine
   Energy
Dagda – Irish Father God
Herne – British God of Vegetation, Vine and the Wild Hunt
Holly King – English God of Winter, Rest and Withdrawal
Brahma – Hindu Creator God
Oak King – English God of Summer, Expansion, Growth and
   Activity
Govinda – Sikh Preserver and Protective Father
Lugh – Celtic God of Smiths, Artisans and Harvest
The Griffons – Mystic Beings, Half Lion, Half Eagle
Old O'Shea – King of the Irish Bearded Dragons. Friend of
   Dagda
Barack – King of the Indian Red Breasted Dragons.

Of the same thought As Pan:

Pan – Greek Horned God of Nature, Shepherds and His Flock,
   Wild Forrest and Fields, Virility, Fertility and Spring
Hephaestus – Greek God of the Forge, Technology, Craft,
   Sculpture, Fire and Volcanos
Anubis – Egyptian God of the Dead
Loki – Norse God, Shape Shifter and Gender Changer. Father of
   Sleipnir
Set/Seth – Egyptian God of Chaos
Eros – Greek God of Sexuality and Fertility
Hermes – Greek God of Boundaries, Travellers, Shepherds and
   Cowherds, Orators, Writers, Poets, Invention, Commerce,
   Thieves and Tricksters, Messenger to the Gods
Durnap – King of the Dwarves

Hounds of Hell – Hades Hounds
Krenaps – Horrible Little Gremlins. Work for Seth
Death Breathers – Called from the Deepest Fiery Pits. Work for
   Hephaestus
Grenlar – war loving mercenaries.

CHAPTER I

A SMALL HOPE

Danby Darello was a typical child. Not tall in stature, yet not small to the eye. He rode a bike and went to school. A typical lad, but for one thing! As his grandmother would say, "that bloody helmet. If he ever takes it off, you'll find there's a bloody disco going on under there!" But we will come back to that.

Danby lived in the little seaside village of Saltburn on the northeast coast of England with his mother Helen, grandmother Stella, great-grandmother Agnes and the twins Fix and Oscar in a big seven-bedroomed house overlooking the sea. He and his family had been forced to live with the two aged grandparents due to circumstance. Danby's father was *the* Danby Darello. Famous for his death-defying acts of courage as a professional ex-sports fanatic but more known globally as the number one Moto X Champion four years in a row.

Danby and his family had no real home to speak of as they had spent the last seven years travelling the globe with their father and being home-schooled by their mother Helen. Life was good for the Darellos until the Black Hills Endurance Challenge eighteen months ago, a fully televised Moto X event organized in the American Black Hills. The first one ever, and only the top twenty riders on the planet were invited to compete, unusual for the sport.

It was June twenty-seventh and the twins' fourth birthday. The family were staying in a chalet just a few miles from the track and were up early to celebrate the twins' birthday as Danby Senior only had a few hours before the race.

The twins burst into Danby's room, screaming, "Danby, Danby. Wake up Danby! It's today Danby. It's our birthday," bouncing excitedly all over his bed and waking him up.

Danby got up and enjoyed a family birthday breakfast and had a fun time playing with his two younger siblings before being told, "It is time to get ready. The race starts in a few hours."

On returning to his room Danby made a horrific discovery. Laid on the floor by the dressing table was a wooden box which contained a wood carving of a Yamaha 250 motorbike that his father had won his first ever race on. His father had sat and carved the bike himself and spent months perfecting it just in time for the day of his birth. Danby was devastated.

"MAM, MAM," he screamed, running out of his bedroom in floods of tears "The twins. They've broken it. Mam, they've broken it."

Trying to calm him down his father took him to his room and sat with him until he was calm enough to explain what had happened.

"They knocked it off and broke it Dad."

"Accidents happen son." His father was a very calm man and tried to explain to Danby that the twins were young and didn't mean it!

"It took you ages though dad. You told me!"

But his father tried to explain. "It might have taken a long time to make and it might take a long time to repair. But I promise I will have it back to new for you!"

But Danby was ten. He did not understand. All he knew was it was his and the twins broke it! "I'm not going!" He cried. "Why do you always take their side? It's not fair! I am staying here!"

Danby Senior thought it would blow over and Helen agreed that she would stay home with the three of them and would see him after the race. Before he left he kissed Helen, Fix and Oscar goodbye but Danby would not acknowledge him. Danby senior just smiled, blew a gentle kiss and left. That's the last time they saw their father.

About three-thirty the next morning Danby was awoken to the sound of his mother's sobbing. Upon leaving his bedroom he was greeted by his mother and his father's two best friends, Stan Milburn and Chris Knapper. The family had known these men for years as they followed the Moto X circuit as keenly as his father did. In fact, Stan is Fix's godfather and Chris is Oscar's

"There's been an accident," his mother struggled to say through the tears. "Your father... Please give us a minute? Please son. Go to your room? I'll be there in a minute. OK son?"

Feeling low and with a burning pain in the pit of his stomach Danby found it hard to fight back the tears and slowly made his way back to his room. Pretending to shut his door behind him he stood there and listened to what was said.

"It's funny," Stan said. "I know this isn't the best time to bring this up but they couldn't find his body." Stan paused for a moment and continued "Just burnt and broken shards of what used to be his bike. And his helmet? I do not understand it! Not a mark on it! It is impossible!" He just stood there and shrugged his shoulders.

"What are you trying to say Stan?" Helen asked.

Stan looked at Chris and just simply replied, "I don't know Helen, I just do not know."

The family stayed around the Black Hills for nearly nine weeks, trying to find out what had happened to Danby Senior. But nothing was discovered and nobody could explain just what had happened. The body had just vanished. By this time Danby had started cutting himself off from his family and the other people around him whilst living his life in his dad's helmet. Strangely enough, the couple of months after his father's death he began to refuse to remove the helmet for any reason whatsoever! Psychiatrists, doctors, friends and specialists could not talk him out of it! Danby was certain he could find out what had happened to his father but as time went on he started to lose all hope. Once the money had started to run out Helen had no other option but to give up the search! Helen's mother and grandmother were still alive and living in England, so Helen decided to take Danby and the boys to stay with them, as she tried to work out what to do now and how to bring three kids up on her own.

Agnes and Stella were a loving, funny pair, but a couple of old-school English ladies, with rules and a stern temper. Stella was an understanding woman besides her stiff upper lip and fuddy-duddy attitude to life. She had lost her husband and Helen's father years ago whilst Helen and her younger brother Caine were both barely teens. Their father James was a deep-sea diver and was a hulk of a man. One day on a job in the Persian Gulf he just never resurfaced. That was the last they heard of Stella's husband.

Helen's brother Caine had joined the British forces and was at this time serving the people of Britain in Afghanistan. The family was so very proud of Helen's brother. Agnes and her deceased husband Tom helped bring up Helen and Caine after their father James was taken from them in the unfortunate diving accident. James was a stern man with little to say. But what he did say, he truly meant. A meticulous man with a space for everything and a lover of all things green and living, spending most of his time at home tending his vegetable patch and garden.

Agnes was a very strict woman with old fashioned values. Wise enough in years to be able to twist whatever subject arose to benefit her. An intelligent woman who took no nonsense, but if you got to know her, Agnes had a wicked sense of humour and loved to dance. Never a drop of alcohol or packet of cigarettes was ever to enter her house, as she saw drugs and alcohol as the root of all evil. But despite their sometimes stuffy attitude and set ways, I think they were both glad to have their family with and around them. And if I may be bold enough as to presume, I think that big house may have been large and cold without a family. The only thing missing at the moment in the household was laughter!!

CHAPTER II

YOU DESERVE AN EXPLANATION!

Danby had been at his grandparents' home for about thirteen months now and was enrolled in school, but was never accepted by the other children, who taunted and bullied him. Some might say that the wearing of a helmet twenty-four hours a day might seem a bit strange. Well yes! It is! And everybody else thought so too. But Danby was not bothered by this as he was just drawing deeper and deeper into himself, whilst removing himself from everybody else. Everyone else, except for the one person he found he could talk to: Agnes, who by her own admission "never judged and only gave out advice if she felt she was of adequate knowledge, to come to a fair and fully informed conclusion". The problem being Danby felt it was somehow his fault for being angry on the day of the accident. Like somehow karma had intervened and thrown a devastating blow. And adding to that, the fact he felt strangely let down by his father for breaking his promise and not returning from the race to repair Danby's carving. At this time Danby was feeling sad and so, so alone.

Agnes woke Danby at five-thirty one morning, with a cup of tea and two slices of toast with thick lashings of butter and strawberry jam. Mainly in the centre of the toast: obviously bread in the good old days came in round loaves? It was still dark outside and the large house had not started to heat up yet. Still half asleep and decidedly puzzled, Danby asked, "It's only five-thirty gran. Why am I up? And you have never made me breakfast before."

Agnes smiled, walked towards the door and turning her head before leaving told him, "Well son it's quite simple. I have had enough! I have sat for over a year now and watched you in your room, day after day playing games on that bloody tele gamers electric boximeejigggee and nowt said owt! Well I promised I would never give you a hard time over that silly hat of yours. But you are getting fresh air through the bloody thing! I have lived in this village all my life and in my time I have got to know a few people and a friend of mine owns the local newsagents, so I went out and got you a paper round, now get up and I suggest yer wrap up some. It is cold out. See yer down stairs."

Danby struggled to tear himself from his comfortable warm bed and finally getting up dragged his duvet with him towards his neatly folded clothes sat in the corner on an old rickety chair. He started getting dressed very sheepishly and made his way down stairs to find Agnes wrapped up and waiting by the coal fire. "Ready then?" she asked, and then proceeded to walk out the door. Danby quickly put on his hat, coat, scarf and shoes at record pace to keep up with this light-footed eighty-four year old!

When he got out the front door, Agnes was nowhere to be seen. Danby frantically ran around the corner looking for her and there she was, already three-quarters of the way up the long, dark street. Danby ran to catch her up, shouting for her to slow down and wait. Which she never did. On catching up with this nimble old age pensioner he quizzed her on why she wouldn't slow down and wait for him?

Her reply was delivered blunt and simple: "I am eighty-four years of age and what makes you think I have time left to wait about for young, healthy teenager?"

Agnes proceeded to take him to Saltburn Square, near the railway station and only five minutes' walk from home. She was taking him to see an old friend of hers who owned the newsagents. He had owned it for nearly forty years and took it over from his father who took over from his father...... Blah, blah.

Mr Green who owned the newsagents was a funny looking man, about five feet and two inches with a rather round body and an unusually long neck. The strange looking man had beady little eyes, looking constantly over the top of his glasses, whilst raising his eyebrows and top lip to reveal his teeth when concentrating! Mr Green's a merry soul, though, always a smile on his face and a sweet box by the till for the small children. He somehow saw the newsagents as his calling in life. A good honest job which gave him the chance to meet new people and keep him in touch with those he had known for any length of time.

You heard Mrs Green quite a lot but no one had ever seen her. Apparently she was a beautiful woman in her day but after getting married she reportedly made herself comfortable in front of the television with a box of sweets and has followed that routine to this day. Apparently she couldn't get out of that chair now even if she wanted to, as all that sitting down and all those sweets have taken their toll on Mrs Green and turned her into a very large lady, as Agnes calls it Mr. Green would just smile and say, "She's happy." His shop was like an Aladdin's cave to Danby, with sweet jars everywhere, most of which Danby had never even heard of, boy's magazines and an old till, that amazed Danby as it had no lead to plug it in and worked as if by magic. He thought to himself that he might enjoy working here.

Danby had been working his paper round for several weeks now and enjoying it, which helped as he had promised his gran he would stick to it. Whilst starting his round on Ruby Street, one cold and dark morning, riding his bike to deliver his first paper, he heard a noise that made him turn around and look. At this a stone hit Danby and bounced off of his helmet. Danby could not see anybody. It was early and the streets were barren. He started back on his way and another stone hit the back of his left shoulder. He spun around quickly but still no one was there. He had a good look all round him and set off back on his way. As he turned he heard sniggering and not knowing where it was coming from he shouted out, "I can hear you laughing and know where you are so you might as well stop being silly and come on out!"

There was a short silence and then another stone came flying towards Danby, but this time he had seen the arm that had thrown it. "I have seen you, stop being a muppet and come out!"

At that Reece Eggett and his mates Curtis Ravanelli (Rav) and Terrence Crook, the school bullies, appeared from around the corner and proceeded to chase Danby onto the beach. Danby rode faster and faster, trying to put some distance between him and the bullies who were on foot, but found that once he rode onto the beach he had no grip or real control of the bike. He threw his bike and papers to the floor hoping that Mr Green and his Great-Gran would understand because he was in real fear for what they were going to do to him.

Fear took over and Danby ran and ran but did not dare to look around to see if the three were still in pursuit or had given up, and just kept on running until he reached the pier. Once there Danby collapsed with exhaustion onto one of the big supports holding the old pier up, and on turning around to see if the bullies were behind him felt relieved to see Reece, Rav and Terrence walking away in the distance riding his bike and throwing around his papers. Danby did not take this well and ran in tears towards the cliffs. With everything that had gone on, the one thing he had in life that let him escape a little bit and feel useful, was in danger of disappearing when Gran and Mr Green found out what happened to his papers and that they had not been delivered and all because of a few thoughtless idiots.

Feeling down and depressed Danby headed for the cliffs with his head sank low, flicking sand with the toe of his shoe as he walked. Once at the base of the cliffs he decided life was getting just too much for him, plus adding the fact he was missing his father deeply, Danby thought I could be with him! Sitting on a large rock at the foot of the cliffs and feeling sorry for himself for some time now Danby stared at the water surrounding him. With a split-second decision Danby jumped into the sea and was amazed to find that the water moved around him and would not so much as wet him. He walked out farther and farther and the water just swirled around him. He was confused and mystified. What was happening? Danby just kept on walking farther and farther out but the water would not touch him. Like when you try to push two magnets together at like poles and they push each other away.

Am I dead already? Danby thought to himself whilst pinching the back of his leg. "Ow? Well I felt that!" he said to himself. At this there was an almighty flash of the most beautiful blues, greens and the most brilliant white light that just absorbed the body and made you feel warm and safe. As the light came closer you could just start to see the shape of a woman's body.

As she approached Danby noticed that her gown was made of what can be best described as soft swirls of the bluest, purest water gently flowing over her and forming a grand robe, whilst her hair seemed to be made up of vegetation. Yet she was the most spectacular and beautiful sight that Danby or anyone had ever seen. She beckoned Danby towards her and he did her bidding without question, as the aura she was emitting was so calming and peaceful it made Danby forget all about his worries and problems and make them all just float away. Danby walked straight towards the strange figure, the sea parting with every step he took.

The mystical figure held her hand out and took Danby's. At this the figure slowly turned around and headed back to the foot of the cliffs. As they approached the foot of the cliffs the same beautiful light appeared just as radiant and inviting! You could just make out the cliffs parting deep inside the light, to reveal the most amazing palace floating in what seemed to be never-ending blue skies, with the occasional scattering of cotton wool clouds and waterfalls from all around it. A strange but cooling breeze that filled you full of energy with a scent of something magnificent he had never smelt before.

"Where am I? Who are you?" he asked. But the beautiful apparition just put her finger to her mouth – "Shhhhh" – then beckoned him to follow her. Danby had a strange feeling of inner peacefulness and could sense that he was safe with this magnificent and magical figure. But it's a feeling Danby was secure with!

CHAPTER III

THE INTRODUCTION

The enchanting figure led Danby into the cliffs, and once inside they magically closed behind them. Ten feet in and the ground just disappeared, nothing but blue sky and the most amazing palace just floating there in front of them.

"But how? This is just not possible! Who are you? What do you want with me?" At that a giant galleon made from what appeared to be water and clouds, whilst seemingly powered by thunder and lightning, with beautiful golden masts, and sails woven from the finest silks and gems.

A giant white unicorn adorned the front of the boat and silken ropes in its rigging. How did something this big appear from what seemed to be nowhere? Danby asked himself, not wanting to bother the figure with silly questions. Amazed, Danby climbed on board the ship and was shocked to find the thing steering the vessel was what would appear to be half-monkey and half-man, with red trousers and waistcoat braided in gold and with a golden tiara type crown which looked to have been pressed on. A cheeky grin with a definite glint of mischief in his eyes.

"Danby. May I introduce Lord Monkey?" said the figure, as the boat departed towards the magical palace, a strangely beautiful music, very slight and seemingly in the back of his head, started to play. Like a hundred different creatures singing in harmony. It was the single most beautiful and relaxing noise Danby had ever heard!

The radiant figure turned to Danby and said in a soft voice, which felt warm and enchanting, "You are owed an explanation. All will be disclosed to you at the introduction."

As they reached the palace Danby noticed the sound of soft running water, which did not make sense as the fierce 360 degree waterfall cascaded from the palace floor would surely make an almighty roar. And the warm inviting breeze that hugged you like your own mother at birth. Breath taking!

Once passing through the courtyard he was led down a great corridor full of all gods' creatures. Once at the end of the corridor, they were greeted by an enormous arch, which led to an amazing hall. The great hall had the feeling and appearance of clouds and sky, yet firm underfoot like gravity did not work its magic here, and with no walls to speak of; it seemed never-ending, with the feeling of enclosure. Like a world inside a world. A giant table and chairs made entirely of vegetation yet formed in the shape of the finest furniture, living and breathing with an ancient yet connected way of communicating with the strange woman.

The figure asked, "Please. Our other guests are arriving," whilst lifting her hand and gesturing for Danby to take his seat. The figure sat adjacent to him. At that, in walked a strange little man that looked one thousand years old and, with a miserable look about himself, managed to give off an air of calm and nobility. "I shall be announcing their majesties shortly, your highness," he said not taking his eyes off of Danby.

"We are ready to receive, Fargle my loyal friend. Let the introductions begin!"

One by one strange and mighty people emerged from nowhere. Enormous beings, strong and powerful-looking with an air of mystique and a strong look of grandness about them. Gods of myth and legend. The Celtic god Cernunnos with his best friend Herne, the ever entertaining Dagda, the English god of summer, The Oak King, Lugh, Govinda and Brahma.

"No one at this present time can locate and therefore awaken the Holly King your majesty," said Fargle in an apologetic but firm voice.

"Thank you Fargle. Leave us now," the beautiful figure instructed him. Fargle just put his hands by his side, nodded and disappeared as quickly as he had appeared. "Please take a seat my friends?" the figure said. All the gods and deities were seated while our young hero just sat there wide-eyed and wondering what the hell was going on?

The beautiful figure addressed her fellow gods and deities, and said, "Now we're seated I think it's time someone explained to our young helmeted friend just what's happening," and, turning to our young hero, added, "You must be beside yourself my brave young man. I am of a name you cannot understand, yet your people have named me by many names. I think the one you will know best is Gaia or Mother Nature. I am an ancient being who gave birth to this beautiful planet. And as a mother find it hard not to also be its protector. As its mother I have certain responsibilities and may never leave as it will without a doubt cause the end of the world and mankind." At that she smiled at Danby and said, "Let me explain what's happening!"

At that the surroundings changed as to show the past and visually recreate the story Mother Nature was trying to tell. "Roughly one hundred and twelve years go by in the realm of the gods to one of your mortal years." (Approximately one and a half hours of our time, to one week of theirs.) "And aeons ago, nearly two and a half thousand years ago in your mortal years, there was a mighty god who controlled the heavens and my heart. Davqie was his name. He was a just and soft-hearted god with a love for mankind. At that time the heavens had humans evolving on most of the planets in your known solar system. Davqie lived on a floating island, on which he used to travel the heavens and watch over them. About 80 of your mortal square miles wide, it sat in the heavens protecting and preserving every living thing and we would spend so much time together. Our love was so strong but a magic older than us meant we each had to leave our powers in our own realms, before entering each other's. Foolish in your day of man, but back then people had just invented the wheel and we thought our realms unreachable. There did not seem to be any risk. I

23

gifted Davqie an ancient oak, called the Oshaki Oak, as a sign of my love and emptied it of any powers so it would grow and thrive, giving out oxygen and filling anyone around it with simple joy. Davqie decided to use the tree as a place to safely store his power when visiting me in this realm. This tree and magic may never be touched by the hand of mortal man or all will be lost. A warning older than time itself! Hundreds of feet hovering above the entrance to my realm, no mortal man can reach it. In return, my love gifted me a statue of myself made from the stars themselves. Yet with the evolution of man a monster evolved alongside him. Greed. Unfortunately this monster was stronger than ever in a man named Elijah. An untrustworthy thief and liar who would have children, just to make money from or sell into slavery if the fancy took him. With women aplenty and his offspring scattered across the country it was an inexhaustible way of making wealth. After being chased from a pagan ritual for trying to steal the villagers' gold, Elijah ran from the village, where now stands the place you now known as Kirkletham. Elijah ran and ran like the coward he was. Heading straight for the beach and towards the cliffs. Davqie was just arriving when Elijah saw him and watched as the cliffs closed behind him. After sitting and watching Davqie's and my movements for several weeks, Elijah headed south and patiently waited month after month listening to rumour after rumour until he came across a herd of migrating flying horses. Arrogant yet mighty, elegant horses with flight. thought to be impossible to capture. They will toy with you whilst you're trying to catch them, pretending to let you ever closer. Taunt you for hours as if to punish you for even attempting to capture these magnificent beasts and then just take off when they are bored and of the belief they have taught you a valuable lesson! But Elijah had thought of this and nothing else but this. Elijah's greed just grew stronger. He spent the coming months sat waiting, spinning a web across the floor covering it with scatterings of dust, leaves and foliage so that when the mighty winged horses stepped into it, Elijah would push a large rock attached to the web off of a height, to pull the web tight and trap their feet. The plan worked perfectly as Elijah caught three mighty and magnificent winged horses that day." Her voice started to break as if fighting back tears! "He killed the other two!

"Elijah flew straight back and waited weeks for Davqie to return on his magnificent floating island, and leave it to come see me. The very second that the cliffs closed behind him, Elijah flew immediately up to Davqie's kingdom, at which he could see a glorious glow irradiating from somewhere on the island. Elijah knew this was no mortal prize, and to be visible over every inch of an island this size, it must be something really valuable. It was obviously the Oshaki Oak with all my love's strength he could see. Once reaching the island Elijah was fixated on this magnificent light radiating all these good feelings. Most mortals, even those cursed with evil would have thought of this as pure heaven, but not twisted and greedy Elijah; he just thought of profit. Elijah reached out and touched the tree hoping to break a bit off, but in an instant all hell broke loose! Davqie in a meteoric explosion was thrown back to his own realm sending shock waves around the universe as he was ripped from my realm. Tsunamis covered half the planet and all humanity ceased to exist on all other planets, which became the lifeless orbs as they are known to you now. The tree went up in a massive ball of light that lit the heavens themselves. Stars went out and planets exploded. My love was no more. The strength of our love and the old magic is all that saved this planet we believe.

"What happened to Elijah?" Danby asked.

"Elijah was thrown back to earth, cursed to walk the planet forever, whilst never to feel happiness or love again! He's still out there somewhere, Where? We don't know Mother Nature replied.

CHAPTER IV

SO WHY AM I HERE?

"So, why am I here?" Danby asked.

At that Fargle reappeared and announced, " Aput is here on behalf of Zeus! And he wishes to know what is going on."

"Please tell Aput to inform Zeus we have just located the child and to please give us more time to try and explain what's going on to him? Zeus will understand. Of that I am sure."

A quick "Yes your highness," and Fargle was gone again in a flash.

"What is he?" Danby asked.

Mother Nature giggled to herself and said, "Fargle? He's a Wickon. One of my subjects. Fargle and his people have been my friends for thousands of mortal years. Myself and the Wickons have a simple yet strong bond between us, as they help tend to my needs and in return I tend to theirs. They are an old and wise race from the magical realm of Lingfeln deep in the bowels of the planet. Beneath volcanoes. Home to bitter and twisted tyrants, in a beautiful land surrounded by evil and misery. For thousands of years the dark forces that surrounded Lingfeln kept knocking on its door, but could never get in thanks to a kindly old magician that was at one time ambassador to the mortals and protector of wisdom, truth and courage. That wizard's name was Merlin, a true and genuine friend to me, until about sixteen hundred of your years ago – the time of Arthur Pendragon's demise and transportation to Avalon. One of the surrounding lords, Heriohosis made a deal with Anubis, and in return for his eternal service and his promise to obey his every command, Heriohosis's was awarded the might and elegance of his Death Breather army. With the help of the Death Breathers, the enemies of Merlin had become too powerful for him to ward off. The Wickons were put into slavery and Merlin's name was uttered no more. So Fargle lives with me now as my right-hand man." And with a comfortable and grateful look on her face and gently nodding her head, she added, "But most of all, he's my friend."

Mother Nature then with an unexpected shout clapped her hands together and said loudly. "NOW, back to the matter at hand. Why are you here? Over the last hundred of your years the gods have been watching and reeling at the destruction you humans have imposed upon this beautiful green planet. Pollution, genocide, oil spills, demolition of vegetated areas… The list goes on. You are destroying your own home and none of my other creatures are capable of destruction at the rate you humans are! Until recently we all believed that the Oshaki Oak was completely destroyed but certain events have caused us to unfortunately re=think that conclusion. We now believe a small shard fell into the North Sea and cooled before it could completely burn up. Many gods have split from us and taken a different path, led by Pan, the Greek god of nature. They believe the only way to stop total destruction is to find this shard and pollute this planet, making mankind de-evolve. They plan to set up base in Great Britain as it is an island with just enough inhabitants, after losing a few in the time to come, to fill their needs. And surrounded with icy cold waters, which therefore makes it the perfect place to execute their plan. The plan is to cover all the existing land on the planet with a magical bamboo. This bamboo is an ancient plant older than the gods themselves. If the shard is injected into the bamboo at any point the battle will be over and mankind will go back to pre-historic man. The few that are left on this island will be used as their slaves and worshippers. I have tried to warn you all by throwing natural disasters at the biggest problem countries – tsunamis in Asia, freak storms in the Americas – but nothing ever stops human progress. Not even the destruction of the planet on which you live. It really is sad!"

"So why do you lot not agree with Pan and the other gods?"

"Oh we do as far as you have to be stopped! Only you humans are capable of such stupidity!" Shaking her head, she continued in an elevated voice: "I mean, you as a race have even managed to pollute the air you breathe whilst shutting off your own supply bit by bit and then you go and litter the beautiful sky above your heads with what you yourselves call space litter. And all this caused by those you call the intelligent and powerful? Fools and jokers from what we have been seeing." Lowering her tone to a more calming level she added, "But we believe that mankind will overcome and correct their problems before it's too late. We have faith in your race, shall we say!"

Danby asked again: "So why me?"

"Why do you wear that helmet Danby and why will you not take it off?"

"I don't know," said Danby. "I suppose it's because it hides me from outside. It makes me feel safe! I just feel like I wouldn't be safe if I took it off!"

"There is good reason for that Danby," said Mother Nature. "When the Oshaki Oak tree exploded all shards were believed to have been burnt before they hit the ground. It is now believed that a small shard fell to earth and cooled in the oceans before it could completely combust. We now know the shard was found by one of your ancestors and passed down the line son to son. How anybody came across such an insignificant item we don't know. But obviously they did. Since receiving this information we have had to change the way we think and we now believe that there is a very good possibility your father may still be alive, taken away by Loki and Hermes, Pan's left and right arm! But the shard's old magic and couldn't be teleported as easily as Pan and his people thought. That is why there was no damage to the helmet after the crash. It still gives out goodwill and as a result your family, have kept it as a mere good luck charm, unaware of just what they have had in their possession. That is why after receiving it from his father Danby Senior pushed it deep inside his helmet for good luck. As well as Pan there are those that now believe that is why we are all still here. A small piece of the tree exists on, as does a small remaining piece of the universe. We gods don't hold much stock in mortal superstition or coincidence! We now believe if the shard burns or is somehow destroyed the destruction of Davqie's universe will be complete. Do you now understand how important it is that you must keep the shard safe?"

At that Brahma stood up and shouted with a tear in his eye, "We cannot let this happen. Every time you people destroy something one of us feels the pain. It would be easy to join the others. Death and destruction is all you people spread. Please? Do not let us down."

Danby jumps up. "It's OK. You can have it. I don't want it any more." And with that he started to take off his helmet. For the first time in a year and a half, the helmet was coming off!

"Stop," cried Mother Nature. "You can't take it off here. We don't quite understand what is letting the shard into these realms, we believe it has somehow connected with you and releasing a magic we do not know of, but if any of Davqie's magic is left in the shard and it is removed from you inside one of the magic realms it could be the end of all that is! I am sorry Danby. We just do not know what will happen. I am afraid it's up to you now. And to be totally truthful with you Danby we don't know what happens now. Until Pan makes his first move, we cannot retaliate. All we do know is you are important to the outcome and you must keep the shard safe until our investigations can reveal what the others' plan is! Until then Danby we will try to keep you safe as much as Zeus will allow. Be brave my young warrior!"

"So where is my father?" Danby asks.

"We don't know. There are rumours that they are holding him close, awaiting your arrival. Loki and Hermes were shocked to find the shard missing after the abduction and left Pan rethinking his plans. Pan will still need him if he can get his hands on the shard. I am sure he's safe for now!" Mother Nature reached inside her spectacular robe of what looked like gentle running water and brought out a tiny little creature.

Danby thought the creature was adorable. It was only about eight inches high with short black and brown wiry hair and looking like some genetic cross-experiment gone oh so right.

There in front of Danby stood a chubby eight inch monkey with a pig's snout. "Aw, he's mint. What's he called?"

"This is Mackschmee. He is a Schmee. One of the most ferocious creatures known to the gods and he is to accompany you home in case Pan's people decide to pay you a visit."

"You are joking right?" Danby laughed out loud.

"On the contrary my young friend. The Schmee have been the protectors of the gods for millennia. They can morph into whatever you can see in your mind's eye. You think of absolutely any creature in your mind, real or fictional, and as long as you can see it in your head Mackschmee can take its shape. Go ahead. Try." She passed him to Danby who had his eyes closed. In an instant, Mackschmee jumped to the floor and spun like a tornado. This tiny little creature had morphed into a very large and ferocious-looking dragon, standing forty foot high and looking like it had just arrived through the gates of hell.

Danby jumped off his seat. "Wow. Mint," he shrieked! "So did I do that?" Danby closed his eyes again and like a deflating balloon Mackschmee flew around in front of them and settled at Danby's feet in the shape of a polecat. At which and with a satisfying smile Danby reached down and picked him up. Giving him a stroke, Danby said to the Schmee, "I will call you Mack I think. Me and you little fella are going to have some fun together." Looking up at Mother Nature he asked about his father once more. "I am sorry to go on but are you sure that my father's OK and how do I find him?"

"Slowly Danby. Slowly," said a calming voice from across the table: The Oak King. A magnificent man, eight foot tall and huge in stature. A long grey beard to his knees and his skin reflected light like the deepest green emerald "Don't worry. We believe your father to be safe. He is held between worlds in a place where time holds no power. He will have no recollection of events beyond him being taken. Whilst you wear that helmet you do have a small defence against their

30

power. I really am sorry we have to put this danger in such young hands but it appears that destiny has spoken. Remember my young friend, we will be keeping an eye on you and helping wherever permitted, as a war of the gods cannot happen and must be avoided by all costs! We are sorry our little friend Mackschmee cannot speak, but he will certainly let you know when there is danger."

At that, a huge bellowing voice came from the furthest reach of the table. "Remember boy. You are not alone in this."

It was Cernunnos. He was sat cross-legged on his chair with unmanaged thick hair and a big beard. A huge figure of a man with muscles the size of Danby and what looked to be stag's horns. With a horned serpent in his left hand and giant bracelet of twisted gold adorning his neck, body and left hand. But strangest of all: "I mean," Danby was unsure, "but it looked like there was a stag appearing and disappearing behind his right shoulder."

"Remember child! It is not the size of the man that makes him great." And at that he opened his gown to reveal a cascade of bright lights and comets. What Danby could only describe as fireworks going off and the raw power of worlds colliding. Continuing, Cernunnos laughingly bellowed, "It is the heart and soul of the individual that makes him great!"

Danby spent days in the great hall, asking questions and attending great feasts whilst sat with magnificent beings of myth and legend. Danby now felt somewhat more powerful and had a greater understanding of life and how nature works. When it was time to leave, Mother Nature escorted Danby to the entrance in the cliffs. As he went to leave, she took his shoulder and whispered, "Remember my brave young man. You are right to wear the helmet. You will not know when you are in danger, but hopefully Mackschmee will be of some assistance there! Be safe my child and as for now we must let events just run their course."

CHAPTER V

THE OTHER SIDE

Pan and the other gods had not been sat idle over the years. They had spent the time researching the old magic. Luckily there was little to know about this powerful magic which seemed to tie all existence together, but Loki and his partner in mischief Hermes had travelled many magical realms of the old and forgotten, looking for any scrap of information about Davqie and his old magic. fortunately for us there was not much left, and after hundreds of years in the mystic realms they had only managed to find enough information to grasp a basic knowledge. And that was sketchy at best. Pan had several very powerful allies in Loki, Hermes, Hephaestus, Anubis, Set/Seth, Eros and a sneaky helping hand from Hades every now and again, against the orders of his brother Zeus who had forbidden him to get involved!

Pan and his allies were using the realm of an evil little dwarf king, near the old mines in Eston Hills. Durnap the king of the dwarves was a bitter, twisted soul, over a thousand years old and spending every minute of his time plotting his revenge on the humans. He hated humanity for the evils done to his kind in the past and resented the fact he could not walk the earth with man. Purusha the dwarf goddess agreed with Pan and the others but, out of respect to her old friend Brahma, declined their invite. Despite this, Purusha secretly arranged for Durnap to give the opposing gods a great hall to meet in. Saltburn and Eston are just on the outskirts of Middlesbrough. There were a lot of realms in this area, as Teesside is an industrial, downtrodden town. No fairy tales nor magic and mystery. No golden rainbows or happy ever afters. Just hardened, ordinary people, trying to scrape a survival and escape reality through drugs, drink, violence and crime. Where better to hide mystical worlds than right in front of people with no time for that nonsense? Where children must grow up and fast.

Durnap and the gods were gathered in his great hall! A spectacular room with walls of gold and precious stones, the finest silken tapestries depicting great dwarf battles adorned the great walls. The table in the centre was enormous and of the finest carved marble, with the faces of Durnap's ancestors portrayed so lifelike placed around it. The chairs were of an unusual pattern that seemed to move the deeper you looked into it.

Seth and Anubis were just about to put the first part of the plan into motion. They found it too easy to mess with the mortals, especially since they had time itself on their side. Pan had been putting this plan into motion for over two thousand years. Watching and studying, waiting to see mankind's next move. This translated in mortal years to the early nineteen seventies. Seth was set to play with the world's stock markets and cause global chaos, whilst Anubis was set to send an army of the dead across the planet to plant the ancient bamboo in specially chosen places. This bamboo is no normal bamboo. Once, before the time of man and gods, it was the only living thing in the universe and once planted it covers all land and can grow in any climate, with a tolerance to all poisons and temperatures and if burnt will return twice as fierce. Its only barrier is deep water over three hundred feet deep. One root bowl can cover a whole continent in a matter of weeks, replacing and overpowering everything in its path. The only real option of clearing this threat once it is planted are the gods themselves that plan to plant this curse, as before mankind the gods came and cleared away the bamboo and cleansed the land.

But over two and a half thousand years ago in the mortal realm Zeus decided to reward and ascend a mortal man, a simple but honest chemist to the gods and give him his own realm to stock and catalogue things extinct, extra-terrestrial and currently residing on planet earth. A record of all life ever to grace this planet! This job was given to a Greek named Herophilus's. Zeus chose him all those years ago as he became Zeus's loyal friend and chemist. A mortal that can comprehend the science of the gods, the mystery of the universe and owning an ever-inquisitive mind. Zeus found this most amusing and so promoted Herophilus's to record keeper and official historian of all to the gods.

We hear that Loki and Hermes have just visited Herophilus's in his realm, leaving a wake of confusion and disbelief behind them. The entrance to Herophilus's realm is in Venice, just behind Saint Mark's Cathedral and by his own admission, "It is not far from being submerged." Loki had changed his appearance to that of Zeus himself and conned Herophilus's into showing him around. Loki did not have to try hard to trick Herophilus's as his head was full of artifacts and catalogues. Herophilisus's was a tall slim man with an appearance of an ordinary old age pensioner. He stooped forwards as he could not stand straight any longer and his beard dragged along between his legs sweeping the floor, with an enormous quiff of thinning hair on top of his long thin head. His nose was large and pointy, turning to the right quite sharply as it had definitely been broken at some time, with a large wart and small rimmed glasses with lenses as thick as hockey pucks, balanced precariously on the bridge of his nose, his eyes moving around the sockets not unlike a pinball around a pinball machine. Some may say he could buy his train ticket on one platform and watch his train leave from another platform at the same time! He was a gentle soul, though, and was very easily duped into leading Loki straight to what it was that he was looking for. He only needed the smallest of pieces to bring their plan to fruition! And Loki found it only too simple to get what he was after! On leaving Herophilus's realm, Hermes was waiting on his return. On seeing a nod Hermes burst out in laughter! "LET THE GOOD TIMES ROLL!" he shrieked loudly.

Loki smiled at Hermes with a mischievous and downright evil grin. "So you fancy some fun too then? Shall we play? Hermes smiled a cheeky smile and Loki instantly turned into the pope Benedict XVI in all his finery and started to walk into the square! People everywhere were bowing and making the sign of the cross, screams rang out from those excited by the arrival. Making his way into the middle of the square, touching people's heads and blessing their children, upon reaching the middle of the square Loki looked towards Hermes, who was staying out of sight and excitedly waiting to see what mischief his partner in crime was about to unleash on these poor God-fearing folk. Loki looked to the sky, lifted his hands to the heavens. As everybody started to bow, more and more people turned up.

Loki took a long pause and deep breath, before shouting at the top of his voice: "LORD, PLEASE HEAR MY PRAYER? After a pause of about twenty seconds in which the square had filled to maximum capacity, he continued, "YES LORD HEAR MY PRAYER. AS I YOUR SERVANT AM FOREVER AND FOREVER WILL BE FOREVER," and in a more sinister tone continued on to say: "SICK OF THIS RELIGIOUS STUFF AS THIS POPE FEELS THE NEED TO P-A-R-T-Y!

At that Pope Benedict XVI pushed his way through the crowds, throwing insults at people and walking round throwing food and drink, whilst shouting insults and renouncing Christ, with the by now massive crowds running about bemused and bewildered, not knowing what's just happened. Loki then confused the crowds more by proceeding to remove his robes and reveal what appeared to be leathers and a Hell's Angels waistcoat, with the words "Satan's Angels" in big silver letters stitched across the back. Loki stood there stiff as a board and placed sunglasses on what people believed to be the face of Pope Benedict XVI. With a smug, self-satisfied smile pressed firmly on his face, he went on to light a cigar, lift a finger and made his escape to Hermes waiting nearby. "That was the funniest thing I have seen in a thousand years. You have to love these simple humans. They really believe you're him."

And in fits of laughter Loki screams, "LET THE CHAOS BEGIN!" before the two of them make their return to Durnap's Great Hall laughing and giggling like a couple of naughty children the whole time.

On their return, the mood was high and joy full at the news of their success. Everything was going according to plan. Over in the corner of the great hall, set in a great arch and recessed into the wall, stood a multi-coloured vortex in which time does not exist. This vortex contained the next part of the gods' plan. Danby Senior.

After Danby Senior's kidnapping went wrong, Pan had to think of another use for him and after the appearance of his son with the helmet his only use was obviously bait or blackmail. If these didn't work in retrieving the shard then they would have no further use for him! Danby Senior was in storage until Pan worked out which angle to use on him and to create a plausible story to why he was being stored in there in the first place. Somehow he must also be convinced that the shard is for good and must be retrieved at all costs. But with the time difference between mortal and god realms they were in no rush to awaken him. Durnap and his dwarf people threw an almighty party that night to celebrate and ward off evil spirits from the days to come and the battles to be fought. The party lasted for eight nights and great merriment was had but it came time for the gods to return to their own realms and rest. They would have to be alert over the forthcoming months. D-day being March 2012!! The time was drawing nearer for the gods to teach man a lesson. It was all just a waiting game now!

CHAPTER VI

THE BEGINNING

On returning home Danby found only about thirty minutes had passed. He took a minute like we all would and thought to himself, "Was that real?" But then a polecat named Mack nibbled at his fingers and looked up out of Danby's pocket, winking at him and then scurrying back to his nice warm bed. Danby felt different. He was more comfortable in his helmet and still felt somewhat more powerful and retaining a basic understanding of the workings of the universe. He headed home feeling quite comfortable in his skin but worried about the times to come!

On arriving home he was met by his mother getting the twins Fix and Oscar ready. "You're back son. Everything OK?" Danby tried to tell his mother about his adventure but she just looked at him confused, laughed and asked, "Can the gods help me get these two monsters ready for school as I'm finding it impossible to get them ready on my own? Can you not zap them and make them sit still?" And went about her morning getting the twins ready and preparing breakfast.

Danby ran to see Agnes. "Gran, Gran. You wouldn't believe it Gran. There is a door of light and Mother Nature a light door, and a light door and gods and mon–"

"Whoa...whoa. Calm down horsey... Slowly. It's hard enough to understand you through that ruddy thing as it is. Now what has happened? And slowly!"

At that his mother shouted, "Danby come on, you best get ready. You will be late for school!"

His gran just looked at him as she could see he was about to explode and said, "It will wait. Go to school and I will be here when you get home. Have a good day my handsome boy and we will speak soon!" Danby just smiled and left, but on his way out the door his gran chose to give him some sound advice!

"Danby son."

"Yes gran?" he replied.

She just smiled and said in a gentle voice, "You ever come in this room with your shoes on again my dear boy, I will beat you to within an inch of your life! Do you understand?" Then turned away laughingly saying. "Now off with you and try and have a good day!"

Danby made his way to school through the usual torrent of insults and torments about his helmet but today was different. Danby felt important and didn't pay any mind to the cattle. His days were about to be filled with excitement and danger which strangely made this lot no problem at all. On arriving at school Danby did his usual routine from his locker to his form room. There was something strange going on. A strange atmosphere but Danby couldn't quite put his finger on it. It was one of those "Have you heard?"-type feelings going around the school but unfortunately Danby had no friends to say what have I missed?

Suddenly Paul Metcalfe and his brother Ronnie leaned over and asked. "Have you heard? Mr. Burgess came in to say that our form teacher Miss Milner will not be with us today and to sit quietly until they decide on a replacement. You must have seen him walking out?"

There were kids chattering everywhere about a giant crab which had come ashore in Whitby and had apparently crushed Miss Milner's car as well as many others. And strange talk about Pope Benedict taking a funny turn in Venice, with the BBC news stating clearly that the Vatican can verify the whereabouts of the pope and claim it must have been an imposter! Even I must admit this was turning out to be a strange day! And I am thinking this stuff up! Anyways! Danby was starting to worry. "These ain't no ordinary incidents. Not after what I have just experienced!" At this Mack jumped from his pocket and ran out of the school. When Danby caught up with him he was stood in front of two strange men. The first was a strange-looking man dressed like an old mucky court jester, but he didn't look much fun at all. The second was a handsome man with matching sandals and cap, both with wings. He wore nothing but a toga and with a staff in his right hand and a tortoise in the other. There was also a giant rooster perched on his shoulder, silent and stern.

"Let us introduce ourselves, shall we?" said the first man.

Danby looked down at Mack and seen he was pacing left to right and back again. He did not look impressed by these two strangers at all.

"I am Loki," the jester said as he tucked his left arm into his stomach and bowed. Swinging his arm on the way up towards his friend and continuing to say. "And it is my pleasure to introduce my very good friend Hermes."

"What do you want with me?" asked Danby.

At that he wished without thinking that Mack was a twenty-foot gorilla. At that Mack starts to spin and shake and within a matter of seconds there was a twenty-foot gorilla stood between Danby and the two strangers. Backing off, the second stranger spoke to Mack. "Now, now. Calm yourself down Mackschmee my old friend. We mean no harm. Just tell us where you have hidden the splinter and we'll be on our way."

At that Mack started roaring and waving his massive arms about whilst thumping his chest which could be heard thundering throughout the streets Loki and Hermes circled the pair before Loki spoke again. "We will not strike now child . But keep looking over your shoulder and you had better have your wits about you, BOY!" And at that and with a sinister smile on his face he turned into Danby's grandmother Stella. "Now what about it son? THE SHARD?"

At that Mack with one almighty swing sent Loki into orbit. Spinning round Mack looked at Hermes, who with a defiant smile just vanished into thin air. "Good lad Mack. I suppose that will not be the last we see of them two so we had better head home. We are not going to get very far with you looking like that!" And at that, Danby imagined Mack in his original form and slipped him into his pocket.

When they arrived back home they discovered the whole family sat around the television set watching the news. "Why are you not at school young man?" Danby did not know what to tell his family as he found it all a bit hard to believe himself.

"Erm... Well actually... Erm... It's a strange and very confusing story involving Miss Milner's car and a giant crab?" And looking very puzzled as he said it.

"We know!" screamed his mother. "Giant shellfish and monsters knocking everything out the air and sinking anything that dares go in the water! Whitby's being ripped apart by a giant crab, boats are being sunk by sea monsters! What is going on? That dippy government does not seem to have any answers! Ruddy idiots, the whole damn bunch of them."

"But mother. I tried to tell you this morning."

"What, all that gobbledygook you were stood there spurting out this morning? Nonsense." Looking at Danby confused she said, "You mean you were not just out to wind me up?"

With a sarcastic giggle Danby replied, "Over the last year or so have you seen me joke? Once? I'm not joking. And there is more. I think you better sit down. While with Mother Nature I was told a lot of tales explaining what has been going on and found out there could be a silver lining at the end of it all! Dad could still be alive!"

His mother just stood there motionless and fixated on one spot on the wall before falling to her knees crying and covering her face with her hands.

Danby hugged his mam and told her, "It will all be OK! We need to talk!" And at that Danby sat telling his family the tale of what has been going on, whilst comforting his mother who was struggling to comprehend the news that she had just heard.

CHAPTER VII

IT'S A DREAM! IT'S JUST GOTTA BE A DREAM!

The family sat in the kitchen by the stove discussing the events of the day!

"I am scared Danby."

"Yes me too Danby!" the twins piped up.

"If the television is owt to go on things are getting bad out there! Ruddy politicians! Should pull their fingers out! Bloody disgrace it is! Makes me wonder what we paid our taxes for," Stella ranted, eyes still glued to the television.

"Look, there's something else," Danby said as he reached into his pocket and pulled out Mack in his original form, just as Danby had last imagined him. "Now don't be afraid."

As Danby revealed Mack from his pocket a massive "Aww" came from everyone except from Agnes who had somehow managed to send her false teeth halfway across the kitchen. Screaming with laughter Agnes asked "THAT? Hahahahoohoohoohoo." And holding her sides she shrieked, "That thing? No, no don't? Please? I am gonna wee meself!!!"

At that Danby and Mack looked each other and within seconds of Mack hitting the floor there stood in his place a giant English bull mastiff, slobber and all. "Sod me, it's a ruddy rhino!" shrieked Stella. Danby laughed and made his way upstairs to his room.

On entering his room, Danby discovered a dozen or so Krenaps (what we would call gremlins) sent by Seth to ransack Danby's room and try to retrieve the shard of the Oshaki Oak. On seeing Danby enter the room, the Krenaps instantly attacked him and started tearing away at his clothes and helmet, trying desperately to rip them off of him. Danby kicked and screamed, "MACK, MACK, and PLEASSSSSSSE MACK HELP?"

Mack made immediately for his room clearing the stairs in just one bound, bursting into the room and giving the Krenaps no hope at all, tearing at them and throwing them around the room. Danby kicked and punched, whilst trying to get free. Mack fought them all off. Once the room was emptied of these small and sneaky critters, the pair went on a sweep of the house to make sure there was no one else there. Once they were sure the house was empty and all was back to what could be considered as normal, Danby and Mack sat with the rest of the family in front of the television and watched the day's news and events, trying to make sense of what had been going on.

At this time the whole planet was at war with mystical creatures and an indestructible bamboo that was strangling vegetation and moving across the planet at an incredible rate. The world's best brains were collected in London as this appeared to be the only place on Earth not to be infected, but every time they thought they might have a solution they hit a brick wall. They were all flummoxed as to what was going on. In the air were giant dragons, fast as lightning and without any remorse or coincidence, going by the name of Death Breathers, ruled over by an evil and ruthless dragon named Barrook, with a burning hatred of everything and a desire to turn our world into naught but ash. Barrook and his legions were brought up from the deepest depths of the earth by Hephaestus. Sleek and evil, with their flesh smoking and burning as if made of ash, smoke and fire. Controlling everything in the skies. Thousands of them as Anubis's army of the dead march all over the planet planting roots and causing havoc upon the people of towns and villages who were unfortunate enough to come across them! Hephaestus was also enjoying himself playing with the internet and stock exchanges, giving out false information affecting every corner of the globe, collapsing governments and making companies fold. Sending tankers and aeroplane's to the bottom of the deepest oceans and the side of the highest mountains. Eros was scouring the planet making the wrong people attractive to each other, causing anger, brawling on a massive scale and total emotional distress, like foreign dignitaries having open affairs with the wrong people. This was causing arguments between nations and fights in the streets. Whilst the whole time the trickster Loki was close by and keeping an eye on Danby and his family. Pan's plan was going smoothly and his people where were they should be and doing exactly what they were supposed to do! Unfortunately for our young hero, the only thing left on Pan's to-do list was to retrieve the shard! Looks to me like Danby's life is going to get a whole lot more difficult in the times to come!

Danby sat with his head in his hands and decided that the only course of action was to return to the realm of Mother Nature and ask her advice. Danby made his way to the hall to put on his coat and shoes and on turning round saw Mack was right beside him. Danby ordered Mack to stay at the house and watch over the family in a firm and harsh voice whilst shaking his finger at him in an up and down motion. Mack just shook his head, covering everyone's coats and shoes in slaver, with a good helping up the walls and on the ceiling just for good measure.

Running for the door, Mack managed to go flying on the hall rug across Agnes's freshly polished floor, before ending up in a heap against the front door with a dopey look on his face. "Well it looks like were going together then, eh lad?" Danby finished off putting on his shoes and jacket and they both headed for the wall across the road.

Upon reaching the wall, the pair climbed over it and dropped down onto the beach. Heading for the cliffs where he entered Mother Nature's realm, Mack spotted a number of dark objects emerging from the sand and running out of the sea. It was the hounds of hell. Controlled by Anubis and owned by Hades. Dozens of them all were making their way toward Danby and Mack. Quick as a shot Danby closed his eyes and imagined the biggest dragon he could muster in his imagination and within an instant Mack was the enormous dragon that Danby had pictured in his head. The beast looked even more impressive outside his head than it did in it, with huge claws, a thick armoured skin and an enormous spiky tail. Danby quickly mounted the dragon before the dogs could reach him but the mass of Mack made it impossible to take off before they reached them. Flapping his mighty wings and flicking his tale violently at the dogs, Mack screamed out in pain. There were just too many of them. As our pair fought frantically to escape, the hounds of hell just kept coming. Fighting for their lives and wondering just how they could they could escape the beach, Mack just kept flapping his enormous wings, in an exhausting bid to reach the air, when all of a sudden there was a collection of loud claps and the dogs started to fall off of Mack's enormous frame. Still alive, but dazed and disorientated, this gave our pair just long enough for Mack to take flight. Kicking and flailing his arms about to get rid of the last dog, Danby was in trouble as he was powerless against this impressive beast. The hound edged closer and closer, until all of a sudden Mack started downwards at full acceleration. Levelling off just above the water, Mack pulled up sharply upon reaching the cliffs, spinning his body around and trapping the hound between his mighty frame and the cliffs. As the hound fell to the ground, Danby took a look back to see where the loud clapping noises were coming from. To his surprise, there was Reece, Rav and Terrence waving their arms about shouting out to distract the monsters, whilst stood with a dozen or so fathers brandishing shotguns and an array of antique weaponry. Now that Danby and Mack were safely in the air, the dogs turned on the bullies and their fathers. Danby screamed at Mack to return and help them, when all of a sudden as if from nowhere, three Death Breathers arrived and tried between them to knock our pair out of the sky. Mack took off as fast as he could, flying round and round the cliffs, but unfortunately having to leave their helpers to their own devices. The opening to Mother Nature's realm was not there though! Danby was screaming: "Mother Nature where are you." There was no reply though and the port hole was just not there. Mack was twisting and turning whilst trying everything to evade the Death Breathers, who were spitting out solid balls of pure fire and just missing them on more than one occasion. Danby was hanging on for dear life and things were just getting worse, as on the horizon he could see more Death Breathers arriving to join the hunt. It was time to face the fact that Mother Nature was not coming to their aid, so Mack took off across land trying to avoid the three evil beasts that were in pursuit. Flying as fast and low as he could Mack took off. But it was no use they were too fast. Heading in a south-westerly direction across land, they both noticed a dark shadow in front of them.

As they drew closer Danby and Mack could both make out it was more dragons flying on an intercept course and closing in at a steady rate of knots. This is it, Danby thought, dozens of dragons chasing us and even more in front of us heading our way. It definitely looks like the pair were done for.

"Was an honour to know you Mack!" Danby shouted, slapping Mack on the shoulder as if to give him a pat on the back. But Mack didn't give up quite so easily. The brave Schmee pulled up his head and heading for space, he continued climbing higher and higher! Neither dared look back, as they just rose higher and higher into the sky. Danby's breath started to freeze the higher they got, shivering and with his teeth chattering in the sub-zero temperatures of the upper atmosphere. Once he lost momentum Mack thought to himself, "Well this is it. Let's have it!" And proceeded to head straight down into the awaiting hoards. But none of the dragons seemed to have followed them. Danby was fighting to stay conscious, but still had enough about him to think. Why? They were both confused. As they got closer to the ground they got their answer as they noticed what looked like a great battle between the masses of dragons. The horde heading from the southwest were friends of Dagda and sent on an intercept course to help and protect the pair. It was Old O'Shea King of the Irish bearded dragons, with his royal guards! Asleep for over a thousand years and awakened by Dagda for the sake of a good fight! And Old O'Shea was only too happy to oblige! The pair thought it wise to avoid the fight and carried on in the direction that help had arrived from, keeping as low as possible until they hit the shores of Ireland. Once there, there was a blinding light being omitted from the cliffs, like a guiding beacon and looking like the warm inviting light that was given from the entrance to Mother Nature's realm. It was Dagda and the entrance to his realm. Mack landed and once they knew they were safe Danby returned Mack to his natural form and slipped him back into his pocket.

"Mother Nature said you were heading this way. I have been waiting for you. Quickly inside, we must talk?" Danby walked into the realm as quickly as he could, and as the entrance in the cliffs closed Dagda introduced himself and informed our pair that they were being waited on. Danby thanked Dagda for his help. "I thought we were goners there sir. I don't know what would have happened to us if those dragons did not arrive in the nick of time!" Danby and Mack could breathe easy now. Even if it was only for a short time as Loki was never far behind them!

CHAPTER VIII

THAT LOKI'S REALLY STARTING TO GET ON MY NERVES

Dagda led them through to a magnificent kingdom filled with emerald-green fields and beautiful mini-palaces. The air filled with the sound of a hundred singing birds chirping a melodious harmony. A warm breeze with the gentle aroma of meadows in summer grabbed you and pulled you in. Dagda let out a bellowing laugh; with a gentle swoosh of his right arm, a wondrous castle appeared in the distance. The type every British kid imagines when he plays King Arthur and the Knights of the Round Table. Dagda was one of the high kings of the Tuatha De Danann, a race of supernatural beings that took Ireland from the Fomorians, who were the island's original settlers. Dagda was promoted to high king upon the life-threatening injury of Nuada, his predecessor. Upon walking into the realm a magnificent carriage came into view with what seemed to be a little bearded man with clothes of emerald green in control of it. With top hat, pipe and the cheekiest of smiles on his face, Danby was too embarrassed to enquire whether or not this was a genuine, bona fide leprechaun, waiting to take them to the castle.

It was only a five- or ten-minute walk to the castle and Danby felt the need to clear his head. "If it's possible could we walk the short distance to the castle your majesty? I just need a short time to collect my thoughts." On the way Danby took this short time to reflect on what had happened. He tried to act brave but the truth is it was taking all his strength to stop his legs from shaking and his concentration to keep himself from throwing up.

On reaching the castle Mack jumped out of his pocket and ran straight through the castle gates. Danby looked at Dagda with shock in his face and said, "There is something wrong. Mack's only acted like that when I have been in danger." Dagda laughed loudly and pointed towards the door. There was Mack and another schmee taking turns to pick each up and rotate each other three hundred and sixty degrees. Danby looked confused. "Ha, ha. That is Ma'schmee. Mackschmee's mother. In fact Ma'schmee is the mother of all schmee and the rotating is their way of showing affection. Come, everyone's waiting."

On entering the great hall Danby was greeted by all kinds of mythical beings and gods of legend. "Where's Mother Nature?" he asked as she was missing from the gathering.

"She has gone to see Tyra, Queen of the Griffons and has sent Govinda to talk to Barack, king of the fierce Indian Red Breasted Dragons. We are massively overpowered in the air, land and sea and desperately need all the help we can get. We have gathered creatures from every realm in a hope they will help. Both creatures from your realm and ours. Mother Nature informed me before she left that if I was to find you, I was to keep you safe here until her return as she needs to speak with you. She has been busy visiting creatures in both realms so, I cannot predict her return. I am sorry my young friend but I must place you between times as you will carry on to age at the same rate in both worlds. It is painless! You will step into the vortex and once we pull you out, it will be as if you have not left."

Danby agreed to this as he knew the longer he spent in the mystic realms the less time elapses outside in his own world and the safer his family would be.

On Mother Nature's return she headed straight to Dagda and after five or so minutes she ushered Danby out of the vortex and into a quiet hallway. "That's amazing. It's as if I never left. How long have I been in there?" Danby spurted to Mother Nature all wide eyed and looking full of excitement!

Mother Nature shook her head and shouted, "Look Danby you are in great danger. Loki and his army have followed you here and wait in anticipation of you leaving. We as gods are forbidden to use our powers or fight directly against another god. You have to remember that they are only doing what they think right to protect this planet. They see modern humans as parasites and feel they have to act. These people are our family. But we can introduce you to those you do need to meet. This is why we cannot help you get back through the entrance to your own world and must put your life at risk once more as there are mystic tunnels that tie the realms together. Some beautiful, and others full of dread and danger. These tunnels, like the prison holding your father, hold no time, but please do not dawdle." Holding her hand out flat a humming bird appeared as if teleported into her palm. "This is Chie, the elder of the hummingbirds. He will be your guide through the tunnels as he has travelled these corridors more than any other creature. Be careful though as the tunnels can move."

Looking at Chie, Mother Nature instructed him to meet them at the Griffons' lair whilst the gods took Loki on a merry chase! "Be safe child and be brave. You have been strong and still need to be for a short time longer. At the Griffons' lair we will meet Herophilus's with news. Mackschmee and his mother Ma'schmee will accompany you on this perilous journey. They will share your thoughts and you may find you have to think a bit bigger. Now go. We must hurry! The fight is not yet swinging in our favour."

Danby, Mack, Ma and Chie all set off down the corridor, whilst Danby thought of what dangers lay ahead, if he was to start thinking bigger than he already had. This made him quite nervous! At the end of the corridor was an enormous door, too big for them to open. Danby had a thought and closed his eyes to imagine an enormous elephant. At this Mack and Ma were to change into two identical elephants. Which worked as well on two of them, as it had worked previously on Mack alone. Only problem was they were approximately half the size Danby had pictured in his mind!

Smiling and feeling strangely relieved at this, he looked at Chie hovering about in front of him and said, "Now I know what she meant when she said to think bigger." And winked. The two mini-elephants were adequate to open the door wide enough for them to get through and revealing a meadow with large cliffs a couple of miles into the distance. Chie took off, leading the gang straight for them. Danby closed his eyes once more before following Chie and imagined a twenty-ton black panther, at which Mack and Ma did their thing. With a big smile and feeling quite chuffed with himself. Danby looked at these magnificent cats and thought to himself, "Two ten-ton panthers! Not too shabby at all!" At this the three of them set off following Chie towards the cliffs and hopefully the entrance to the mystic tunnels!

Meanwhile there had been epic battles on the surface. Man against mystic creatures, and man was not doing very well. With the bamboo spreading more and more rapidly it was leaving draught and famine across the planet. This was not the plan but Pan and his people felt that it served their purpose. Hephaestus toying with the stock exchange and internet, which made things almost impossible for the commonest of people to function correctly in their everyday lives. Had the future become so dangerous, that man cannot survive without his toys and gadgets? It certainly seemed this way. Eros was playing with hormones across the globe and forcing the wrong people together, Anubis's armies covering more and more of the planet and dragons patrolling the skies. Scariest of all was the fact that giant creatures were scouring the planet to destroy what mankind regarded to be his greatest achievements. Our hero's got his work cut out and better get a move on!

Mother Nature and the friends of humanity worked tirelessly, moving creatures and animals to different parts of the globe, to try and hold off the onslaught whilst trying to set Loki and his armies a merry dance.

Meanwhile Danby and the others had arrived at the entrance to the tunnels and proceeded to enter. There was a kind of natural light running through these enormous tunnels with a cooling breeze and a salty smell. The four of them walked for what felt like days before finding the first fork inside the tunnels. But they now had four to choose from. Chie flew back and forth between them, confused-and looking erratic, before finally choosing one. The four set off down the tunnel sheepishly and made their way deeper and deeper until they came across a river of what looked to be best described as stomach bile. Throwing an old sweet in that Danby had stuck to the inside of his jacket pocket, the four watched as the sweet instantly disintegrated. "No problem," said Danby.

Closing his eyes he thought of the magnificent flying horses that Mother Nature had spoken of earlier, only bigger. BAM! There they stood. Danby climbed onto the back of one of the horses not quite sure who was who, and they started to fly across the mass of bile, which went on for as far as the eye could see. They were flying for about five minutes, before a strange and noxious smell overtook them. Suddenly there was a mighty POP and with that the bile started erupting into the air and as if that was not bad enough, a strange hum from behind them getting closer and closer. They tried to pick up the pace, but the erupting bile was slowing them down. POP, POP, POP. The eruptions were getting more frequent and that damn buzzing noise was getting forever closer!

Loki had found them. Turning himself into a wasp, Loki had gathered together nests of these evil little creatures. Millions of them and they were all on the trail of our young hero. Thousands of them were being destroyed by the bile, but not enough to make a difference. At that there was a massive eruption right in front of Danby, throwing him and his mighty winged beast into the wall. At which the winged horse fell towards the ground, struggling to stay airborne. Danby's hood was snagged on a rock, leaving him there hanging defenceless with Loki and his army of wasps getting ever closer. Quickly Danby closed his eyes and pictured a fierce fire breathing dragon and got two, though half the size. Danby had thought to himself whilst hanging there that the smaller dragons would be effective for flying through the erupting bile and with the dragons' fiery breath we might have a chance. Danby sent the dragons flying straight towards the wasps. Killing thousands of them, but accidently igniting the bile and placing them in even more danger. Mack and his mother headed back, grabbing Danby and making their way through the fireballs and smoke. Being held aloft in the claws of Mack it got too much for Danby and he passed out with the smoke. When he came round he was laid in a massive bed that felt like he imagined laying on a cloud would feel like. A room of the most enlightening brilliant white blinded him at first but rubbing his eyes, his eyesight soon returned. Danby got up coughing and spluttering and getting into his clothes, which had been cleaned and folded for him and started to make his way out of the room. Upon reaching and opening the door, Danby was shocked to discover what looked like a jungle clearing right outside his room, filled with what looked to be enormous lions with an eagle's head and wings to match. Danby screamed and ran back into his room blocking the door with whatever he could find to pick up.

After a couple of moments there was a knock on the door whilst he was in the middle of building his barricade, and a gentle voice said, "So you're awake Danby? Do not be afraid. The Griffons are friends and they want to help."

At that Danby stood back and thought for a moment before clearing away the barrier and opening the door. "Are you OK?" asked Mother Nature.

Danby just looked at her blankly and said, "NO.........I think a bit of poo came out!" and laughed it off.

"Come; let me introduce you to my good friend Tyra. She is the queen and mother of all Griffons. And an old, old friend to me and the other gods."

CHAPTER IX

LET'S TAKE THE BATTLE TO THEM

The three of them made their way into the jungle-looking hall and Tyra flapped her mighty wings before jumping on to a six-foot ledge and turning like a dog which was trying to get comfortable, before coming to rest. Mother Nature and Danby sat on conveniently placed stones of different sizes, whilst resembling chairs designed in an old rustic manner.

"Tyra does not speak any language you could be capable of recognizing as such. But do not worry, as she will let me know if she has anything to add!" said Mother Nature.

"What happened in the tunnels?" asked Danby.

"You passed out with the smoke," Mother Nature answered. "Probably for the best as you had an amazing adventure fighting off the Cheeves and navigating the razor stalactites and stalagmites of Hades, while the whole time being pursued by Loki and his army of wasps. Chie got you here just in the nick of time as Loki was just about to surround you and attack. But do not bear that any heed as it is in the past and it is the future that worries me at this present time! In your absence Tyra's people and mine have been transporting creatures both big and small to strategic points around the globe and coordinating with all the creatures sympathetic to our cause. There has been a terrible war going on in the mortal world in the weeks you were outside time's reach. But for now you must remain here in safety until Herophilus's arrives and shares what he has learned in his research into the old magic. There is a reason why what is going on with you is tied to the shard. If Pan needs you that badly, then why has he not struck earlier? He obviously knows something we do not and we need Herophilus's research to find out what."

Danby did not argue as he had sat and worked out from his time in Mother Nature's realm that every week equates to roughly one and a half hours in the mortal realm, which meant his family was safe the longer he stayed in this mystical realm. For the first time Danby felt he could relax and steal a bit of time for himself!

In the meantime Pan was deep inside Eston hills with Durnap and his dwarves, about to remove Danby Senior from suspended animation and put the next part of his plan into fruition! On being released, Danby Senior was awoken to a story of woe and destruction. Pan informed him that Mother Nature had somehow coerced his son into the destruction of the planet in disgust at the way mankind was treating her child, the planet he knew as Earth. Good food and drink was made plentiful and Pan added how he saved Danby Senior from the clutches of this mad deranged goddess, before she whisked away his son in a violent battle, mere seconds before he had brought Danby Senior here to his good friend's realm with the dwarves. Pan explained how Danby Senior's family were close, so not to worry. Pan, Durnap and Danby Senior sat and made merry right through the night, while they talked about how they would be able to help each other, and save the unaware Danby Senior's precious son in the times to come! He was starting to believe that these mighty beings were on his side and had only his people's best interests at heart! Danby Senior knew no different!!

Meanwhile back in the mortal world, while Danby was avoiding the Death Breathers, best friends Reece, Rav and Terry were holed up with their fathers and an army of volunteers that had answered Agnes's call for people to help her precious great grandson Danby, and after fighting the Hounds of Hell and Death Breathers off were chased until Agnes called them into the house. They had been holed up there for nearly two weeks now as the dogs surrounded the family home and while the odd Death Breather circled the house from above, keeping a sharp and deadly eye on the activities going on below.

"Why don't they attack? Why just sit there? I don't understand," Stella asked Simon, Rav's father.

"I really, really do not know!" he replied with a blank look on his face as he just gazed out of the window, puzzled.

Danby's rescuers had been sitting pretty this whole time, but the food was running out and Danby was nowhere to be found. Luckily Agnes was a typical British mother and grandmother with a larder stocked to feed a marching army, but after two weeks of this many people in the house, rationing was not even going to help them. Fortunately the electric and water had not been disrupted yet but all supplies of everything else had been halted: gas, food, etc ... Things were getting desperate for the people of Earth and no more so, it seemed, than for Danby's friends and family!

Back in Tyra's kingdom Danby had eaten and gone off to bed. Outside his door Mother Nature and Tyra were sat talking about the events going on and how much pain Pan and his collaborators were causing. Before Tyra wished Mother Nature a good night and laid her head to rest, she stood astride Mother Nature with her mighty wings engulfing the weary goddess, in a way of letting her know she was not on her own. It was clearly apparent to Tyra that Mother Nature was in great pain caused by the carnage happening to her world and hung her head low. But the truth was that it was nowhere near as low as Mother Nature's heart felt at the damage done by man and the destruction being done by her god friends at this time!

After waiting a time for Tyra to reach a sound sleep, Mother Nature suddenly stood tall and walked to the furthest point. And in a firm but quiet voice, careful so as not to wake anyone, she started chanting. "Char took, Tookie, Amay, Tsing, Voleck, Hamahn, Toonay, Fartook, Uni" over and over again until a blinding swirl appeared to her, small at first and gradually getting bigger. Once it was fully developed, she turned her head as if to check that all was right behind her, and at that Mother Nature stepped through making sure that it closed behind her.

The other end of the vortex came out in the courtyard of the most fantastic palace imaginable, perched on the highest peak of a magical mountain and floating above the world, invisible to human and animal alike. Out into the courtyard stepped what looked a lot like Father Christmas but wearing robes threaded in the most precious of gems and metals reflecting the light like a million tiny ants, each with a tiny mirror on their backs, and an air of grandeur surrounding him. Not like the air of grandeur surrounding the other gods, as this man would have a presence even among them!

"Zeus my lord." And bowing her head Mother Nature said, "Thank you for receiving me Father."

"Come my child. Walk with me," said Zeus as he gently took Mother Nature by the arm and started to stroll around the grounds. "I do love these grounds. The flowers are so beautiful and full of life."

"Yes but I need to talk," claimed Mother Nature. "The world is being destroyed and you sit and do nothing! Why?"

Zeus looked deep into her eyes before hanging his head and said while resuming walking, "Simple. It is because I agree with Pan and the others. I love all my children. Mortal and god alike. But even I must admit that I don't think they will learn." Angrily he raised his voice and the sky started to go dark. "Pan's right. Mankind has turned out to be nothing but parasites on that beautiful, once fertile planet. We provided everything they could ever need to sustain life, but for them it is never enough, polluting and destroying everything we gave them and finding themselves still in need of more! YOU! You yourself feel the pain the planets in more than anyone. Why do you fight so hard for these parasites?"

"But they are your children!" Mother Nature screamed back. "Good or bad, it is a father's duty to love and protect his children and not to abandon them when they have done something to upset YOU! YOU HYPOCRITE!"

At that the sky turned black and with thunder crashing all around, lightning danced in and out of the clouds supplying the only light. "HOW DARE YOU SPEAK TO ME......? ZEUS

THAT WAY? YOU NEED TO REMEMBER WHOSE PRESENCE YOU ARE IN!!" he screamed.

"I am sorry father, I got carried away," she said, bowing her head and taking a step back. "But I have faith in these parasites and I believe they can realize the error of their ways and make amends before it is too late. We have to believe. They are our children and I am their mother and I will do everything in my power to save them from Pan and his narrow-minded followers!"

The sky started to brighten a bit and Zeus told her he had had enough of this conversation and it was time for her to return from whence she came. "Please? Before I go one more Question? Danby. What ties him to all of this?"

Shaking his head, Zeus told her. "You are bound to find out some time, as I hear you have that fool Herophilus's looking into it. I knew I would regret ascending that man. But you cannot help but like him ! As you know, over a thousand years ago the last shard of the Osaki Oak was discovered and kept as a good luck charm by a man call Phillypottius. A fine and inventive man... And also," Zeus paused and seemed to go into deep thought before continuing. "my son." Mother Nature looked at him confused and Zeus continued. "You see, I gave him the shard and thought it of little or no significance to others and as it had no real power I thought no one would ever want or even notice it and if ever discovered I would have enough power to solve the problem."

"And now you are not powerful enough?" asked Mother Nature, looking decidedly confused.

"No, on the contrary my child, I hold more than enough power to put an end to this at any point I choose." He paused and bowed his head low, and as he started to turn and leave he continued. "It is sad though, as I never thought I would reach a point where I would not want to! I am sorry, but you asked." At that he clicked his fingers and the porthole instantly opened. "I think it is time you left! I am sorry my dear, but I think I must just sit back and watch how things turn out. It is man's problem now. If Pan wins, your pain will be over. If you win...

I hope man will listen to you and change their ways. I would hate to see time prove you wrong."

Mother Nature looked gently into his eyes with half a smile and left with her head and heart weighing heavier than ever with what she had just heard!

CHAPTER X

NO FATHER! YOU ARE WRONG!

When Mother Nature arrived back at Tyra's kingdom, Herophilisus's was sat waiting with his knees stacked up with files and papers to the point that he could not see over them.

Tyra walked over to Mother Nature, at which point Mother Nature looked at her and said, "Yes, I am OK, thank you Tyra. Is the boy still resting?" At this point Danby was in the world of dreams. "In that case, what have you found out, my old friend?"

At that Heriophilus's stood up and the files went all over the floor. Bent over and peering over his thick glasses he apologized and made a move to pick them up. Halfway through picking them up Herophilisus's spotted a particular file and dropped the rest of them again. Pushing his glasses to the back of his nose, he started to get up, tapping the file and repeating, "Interesting, interesting."

After about three minutes of silence Mother Nature asked, "Well?"

Herophilisus's looked up at her with a shocked look on his face and froze for several seconds before coming back to life, and looking into the files went, "Oh yes, yes." And drifting once more into a trance.

Mother Nature repeated her question in a quite stern manner. "WELL HEROPHILISUS'S? Do you have anything to say? Have you found anything that can help us?"

"Oh yes, yes." And pushing his glasses to the back of his nose once again and staring at Mother Nature and Tyra and back again, continued to say, "Very interesting news your highness, very interesting indeed. I think the reason Pan and his allies have not yet tried to abduct the young sir is because there is a chance, may, somehow erm…" Screwing his face up, revealing his top teeth and peering over the top of his glasses, continued, "Be a descendent of the mighty Zeus himself in all his glory. Him and his father are…"

"I know this already, is there anything else?" Mother Nature interrupted.

Herophilisus's looked straight in to her eyes shocked and bewildered. "Then there's nothing else highness," Herophilisus's stated. At that he bowed his head and made his way out of the room, shaking his head and muttering to himself whilst throwing his arms about.

On his way out Mother Nature shouted to him, "Thank you my dear old friend. I do appreciate your time and if you find anything else out will you please let me know as soon as you possibly can?" Herophilisus's just left his files and continued walking, waving his arm in recognition of what Mother Nature had said.

At that a very sleepy Danby entered the room and asked what was going on. "Danby my child, please sit and let me explain." At that Mother Nature sat and conversed with the pair and explained what had been talked about in Zeus's realm.

"So you see Danby? And after being handed down to the oldest son it has now come into your ownership, at which Pan had to change his plans. You and Mack should return home and allow me time to investigate further. And whilst you are with your family, Pan and his followers can do nothing to endanger them." Mother Nature stood up and ushered Danby to his feet. Looking over at Tyra she smiled and softly said, "Tyra my friend, we have hard and dangerous times ahead of us. I must accompany Danby to my realm of Summerland and then through the porthole to his home. Once through, I will return as we have much to discuss. Until then my friend I wish you well." And with that she bowed her head and started to leave with Danby.

Upon reaching Summerland, Mother Nature took Danby straight to the entrance and began immediately to open it. "Be brave my dear. This will come to a head soon and I only hope to find a solution before Pan." Pulling his pocket open Mother Nature peered into it and whispered, "Mackschmee my friend, look after him and be as brave and loyal as I know you can, dark times are about to befall us and we could all be in grave danger." Mother Nature then bent over and gave Danby a kiss through his helmet, before sending the pair on their way.

Danby made his way through the entrance and, turning left, headed straight for home. Saltburn was surprisingly warm for this time of year. In fact, it seemed surprisingly warm for any time of the year. The beach and sea front would normally be a hive of hustle and bustle in these sunny temperatures, not today though! The place was ghostly. Not a bird in the sky or a human or animal in sight, with only the gentle lapping of the waves stopping the silence from being absolute.

In a split-second the silence broke to someone shouting Danby's name: "Danby, Danby." A voice carried down the beach. Mackschmee jumped from Danby's jacket pocket onto the beach and waited to be transformed, but Danby was confused and was concentrating on the voice.

As Mack stood waiting (very irate and impatient I may add) Danby caught a glimpse of two shapes in the distance. "It's dad Mack, it's my dad" and running as fast as he could, he made his way towards his father and what was now looking to be Helen his mother.

Meanwhile Mack had been forgotten and finding it extremely hard to make any kind of progress in keeping up with his excited young friend. Danby ran straight to his father and jumped immediately into his arms as his mother caught up.

"Dad," and fighting back tears and an explosion of emotions, he spurted out, "What, how, where, but?"

At that his father looked into his eyes, smiled and said emotionally, "Shhhh, calm down son, I am here now," whilst pulling him gently into his chest and softly stroking his helmet with a confused look upon his face. "Can you not take that thing off so I can have a good look at you? How you have grown! I can only have been away a couple of weeks. Tops? How did you get so big?" Danby Senior asked, feeling very confused.

His mother at this time had caught up, shouting at Danby Senior, "I am sorry dear, but we don't have time for this. Have you forgotten what's going on?" At which Danby remembered all that was going on, and in an instant a giant gorilla appeared in front of Danby Senior's eyes, making his way at a rate of knots towards them. Danby Senior grabbed his son and tried to shield him from this mighty monster. "Run son, run," he screamed, trying to get away.

"It is OD Dad, that's Mack. He is my friend," Danby said to him laughingly. "It's OK. Really."

Mack ran straight at Danby's mother with his arms waving and roaring like he was possessed by a demon. Pushing him away Danby looked confusedly at his father and then, making his way towards Mack, asked, "What is going on?"

In a flash his mother transformed into Loki, Pan's mischievous friend. Danby looked at his father, waiting for him to transform into Loki's friend Hermes. But he never. "Danby son, it is me! It's Dad. I need to talk to you. Please son? You have to believe me!" Danby didn't know what to believe and looking at Mack was pleased to see him close his eyes and nod to indicate maybe 'his father' was telling the truth. Danby ran back into his father's arms and asked what was going on. Taking a step back, Danby looked into Danby Senior's eyes. And with a look of disappointment asked, "Why are you with him dad? What's going on?"

It was Danby Senior's turn to look confused and after turning to Loki he went down to one knee and placing his hands on Danby's shoulders said, "Look son, I don't know what's going on. All I know is that one minute I am riding my bike and the next minute I am being woken up in the most fantastic of worlds to hear how you are in danger! Gods and creatures from my wildest dreams and to top it all off, gods and a bloody huge gorilla just appear from nowhere. Look, Pan and his friends seem like nice decent people, ermmm, I mean gods. They told me how Mother Nature and her followers are trying to stop mankind and stories of great battles and fantastic creatures. I was led to believe that Mother Nature had taken you prisoner in the great battle in which Pan and the rest of the gods saved me. I don't know what's going on son. I am just relieved to see that you are OK. If somewhat older."

Danby flew back and looked at Loki. He laughed and said to his dad, "Oh no, that is not what's going on here at all!" At that Loki lunged towards Danby, at which Mack threw him to the floor.

On landing Loki looked towards the sky and while holding his hands to the air, said, "See, I told you it would never work."

And in a split-second Loki was stood by Danby Senior with his arm draped around him. With an evil smile on his face, Loki winked and the pair then vanished before their eyes. Standing there looking shocked for several seconds, Danby span around and, wide-eyed, shouted, "Quick Mack, we have got to get home and check the rest of the family's alright before we go look for Dad." And after transforming Mack to his original shape the pair were once again on their way.

On reaching the house, Danby was shocked to find the three bullies and all those parents that had so bravely rescued him and made it possible for the pair to escape. "What's going on? Why is everybody round here?" Danby asked the crowd in the living room.

Helen flew straight for Danby immediately upon seeing him, scooping him up in her arms and erratically kissing him on top of his helmet. "Oh my boy. My little boy, you are safe. Oh I have been so worried. I am so glad you are safe. You are not to leave this house again until all this is over! Are you hurt? Has anyone hurt you?" She only put him down to reach over and get a tea towel from the table. Putting it to her puckered lips and wetting it, Helen proceeded to mop his face.

"Mam stop. We don't have time. We must go. I saw Dad and he is OK."

"WHAT?" Helen screamed whilst grabbing him by the shoulders and shaking him quite firmly. "What do you mean you seen Dad? Where? Is he alright? What did he say? Where is h..."

Danby stopped her. "I don't know where he is Mum but the one thing I do know is that me and Mack are the only chance he has got. We have to go Mum but first I needed to know you are OK."

"WE ARE NOW!" bellowed Reece's father. "We have been trapped here by monsters for weeks now and they just vanish minutes before our young friend appears. Does anybody else find this strange or is it just me? WHY? That's what I want to know. Will someone tell me just what is going on please?" Standing back, crossing his arms and shrugging his shoulders he just stood there waiting on an answer.

"What are you trying to say?" bellowed Agnes with a sign of contempt in her voice.

"Well you must admit it is a little strange how this house seemed to be watched and patrolled by what can only be called creatures from hell itself and to top it off they do one just as little fella here decides to make an appearance. So I will ask again. Is it just me?"

Everyone in the house had congregated in the one room by this time and were all whispering and muttering between themselves. "It is not our fault." Danby shrieked. "Man has upset the gods and no one person or family is to blame. If you want to throw blame, look in the mirror each and every last one of you. We children are innocent in this, but we will have to pay the ultimate price for our parent's crimes, so don't go pointing fingers as only you know how much you have added to fuel this fire."

Danby just shook his head and informed everyone there that he was just off to get changed and recommended that those who wanted to leave, do so whilst the coast seemed clear. The house emptied slowly and cautiously but was empty of everyone except those who lived there by the time Danby got cleaned up. Helen was sat with the twins in the kitchen, keenly anticipating Danby returning down stairs, and dived at him upon his return. Helen asked, "What are we going to do? You are such a young child, my child, and it is not fair to put such things on such young and innocent shoulders. What can I do? What will it take for me to take your place? Please son just stay here with us where I know you are safe." Helen jumped to her feet and shouted. "As a matter of a fact. I am telling you. You are grounded." And whilst cleaning up rather haphazardly continued: "You will not leave this house until I say you can. Do you understand me? Do I make myself clear young man? Now go to your room!"

Danby just smiled at Helen and took her by the hands. "Mother, I do not want or need any of this for any of us, but we have been thrown into the deep end and destiny seems to have chosen my path for me."

Suddenly there was an almighty flash of light emanating from somewhere upstairs. "What the hell?" Helen asked as she stumbled back onto the dresser behind her.

Danby went straight for his pocket and screamed, "Mack." At which his little friend jumped straight to the floor and in the instant of leaving his pocket started his transformation back to a mighty gorilla. As soon as Mack hit the floor he was immediately making his way upstairs to see what the danger was. And Danby was right behind him. On getting to the bottom of the stairs Danby was amazed to see Loki pinned against the wall by the mighty Mack. "What now? Where is my father?" Danby screamed at the god.

"Please child! Will you please get your smelly monkey to release me? I have information about your father that I think you would want to know." And looking in disgust at Mack and in a very conceited way, asked, "Well?"

Mack swung his head round to Danby as if to say no, but Danby felt that he had to listen to what Loki had to say as he had no idea where to start looking. "Let him go Mack," Danby ordered, "but keep an eye on him and any false moves you know what to do." Mack just looked at him, despondent-looking, and let go of Loki. Never leaving his side Mack just stood there, eyes transfixed on the untrustworthy god. "Well?" Danby asked. "What threat are you here to deliver now, and where is my father?"

Bowing his head and looking at his toes like a kid in trouble Loki whispered something that Danby couldn't make out. "What?" asked Danby.

"I know where your father is," Loki screamed at him.

Looking confused, Danby stated, "I know. And?"

To which Loki replied, shaking his head, "I know that," and hitting his head repeatedly, called himself "stupid, stupid," before spurting out as fast as he could: "Your father is in Asgard. I have to tell you this. Do not ask me why but Mother Nature will tell you this is true!"

Helen was at the bottom of the stairs listening, and upon hearing this started to make her way up the stairs screaming, "My son, and my husband. Why are you doing this to us? You have no right."

Staring at Helen with a childish look of sorrow, Loki disappeared in an instant. Upon seeing this Helen collapsed into a heap on the stairs. Danby hugged and comforted her. "It will be OK, Mother," and taking her hand, told her: "I have to go."

Helen just lay there crying into her arms as Danby and Mack prepared to go. As they walked out the door, Helen shouted, "Please Mack? Look after my boy and keep him safe. Please? He is my big man now." Mack simply gave her a reassuring look and followed Danby out the door.

CHAPTER XI

KIDS EH!!!

Danby and Mack made their way straight towards the cliffs. There was an eerie silence all around them. No kids playing, animals or families making merry and basking in the sun's rays. Danby had come to realize that nothing would ever be the same again. On reaching the cliffs Danby was relieved that the tide was out and standing in front of them, he shouted as loud as he possibly could, trying to make any kind of contact with Mother Nature in hope that she would hear his cries and open the portal into the magical realms. Danby stood shouting for what seemed like hours, always vigilant to the dangers that could be all around them. Suddenly a small spark appeared and exploded into a beautiful flash of colours with the most gladdening of sights at its centre. Danby ran straight to the figure and, with his arms held wide and tears rolling down his face, hugged her for all he was worth. "They have my dad. You have to help me? Please, help me."

Looking confused, Mother Nature took her hand and lifted Danby's head until eye contact was made. "We know all this," she said, looking more and more puzzled.

"No. You don't understand. They have him," Danby shouted. Mother Nature led him onto the galleon which was waiting there for them and told him to collect his thoughts. They would talk upon reaching the hall.

On stepping off of the mighty boat, Danby noticed that Mother Nature seemed to look in pain. "Wait? Please? You are hurt. I can see it. What is wrong? What has happened?"

Mother Nature just smiled gently and told him not to worry. "Sorry, but I am worried. I am not taking another step until you explain to me what is wrong with you. I can plainly see that you are in pain," Danby said firmly whilst quickly folding his arms like a spoilt child that has not gotten his own way.

With a sigh, Mother Nature told him. "With all the damage going on all over my beautiful Earth, It is making me weak." And kneeling in front of him, Mother Nature explained how the hug from Danby took a lot of energy from her. In a way she could not explain, the contact from Danby and the Oshaki shard had drained her further.

"I am so sorry. I did not mean to, I swear!" Danby screamed with a look of shock on his face.

"I know my child. Now. We must talk and I think you need to explain what is going on." Mother Nature started back toward the great hall and Danby just bowed his head and from now on did as he was asked.

On reaching the great hall, Danby found it busy with the hustle and bustle of mighty gods and creatures, both fictional and nonfictional making plans and plotting defences. "I am sorry, but could we please sit somewhere quieter? I need you to answer some questions?" Danby asked.

Mother Nature took Danby by the hand and led him away to the far end of the table and carried on into what seemed nothing but open sky. When suddenly he walked through, what could be described as an inch of water. And on the other side he found himself inside an enormous nursery which must have spanned for miles.

As he Looked about, amazed, Mother Nature told him, "This is where I nurture all of my creations. I am working around the clock at the moment in preparation of what is to follow on the surface of my green Earth." And looking despondent, she took a deep breath and confidently with a strong tone in her voice, asked Danby what it was he was trying to tell her.

Danby told his tale to Mother Nature, who sat there and listened tentatively. "Loki said he has taken my father to somewhere called Asgard and you know of this." He quizzed her.

"I know nothing of what you have just told me and have no idea why he would say I did. Mmmmm. All I can think of is that Loki has been home. Loki has spent an eternity trying to prove himself to his own father, Odin. Perhaps he could be telling the truth. But Odin has sworn not to get involved?" Walking about in deep thought, Mother Nature looked at Danby all inspired looking and said. "That is it. Odin's not getting involved. Loki had to leave your father there. Loki sees Odin and gets a look of disapproval. It does make sense in a twisted type of way. Odin would not interfere, but with no one to open a portal for him, your father would be trapped. Clever. Possibly the last place we would think to look. This could be the break we have been waiting for. Who would have thought that the problems between Loki and his father could be the saviour of you and yours? Come, eat." and leading him back through to the great hall, sat him down and told him to stay positive and relax whilst she went off to make arrangements.

On her return, Mother Nature had a strange-looking woman with her. "This is Doideag. She is an ancient relative of mine from the Isle of Mull. She was the real reason for sinking of the Spanish Armada in 1588. Doideag has agreed to open the portal unto Asgard. You should be safe as we know of no enemies being there. Once Doideag opens the portal you will step through to be greeted by an enormous golden path, heading forever up until reaching Valhalla. Your father will not be accepted into Valhalla as it is reserved for those that have fallen bravely in battle. Once reaching Valhalla, your best course is to search the grounds around the area before descending another golden path to Asgard. This is a long and could-be perilous journey as we cannot see inside Odin's kingdom and have no real way of knowing what awaits you. Well, it is up to you once again my little hero. But I am sure your father would understand if you choose not to accept this challenge, with all you have already been through."

Danby just simply smiled and replied, "I think we both know that I have to do this," and nodded to Doideag that he was ready to begin.

At that Doideag proceeded to make a large circle with a smaller one in the centre out of salt. The space between the circles was split evenly into four sections with four lines drawn from four ghastly-smelling powders. Doideag then proceeded to take out five items from an old, large, leather sack and began to place them one by one and kind of introducing each item to the circle as she went along. In the top left section she placed firstly the Andvarinaut ring, a magical ring which is said to have the power to create gold. In the bottom left she placed the horn of Beowulf. In the bottom left and pointing into the centre she placed the Naegling, a magical sword and family heirloom of hrothgar, gifted to Beowulf after defeating Grendel's mother. In the bottom right section, facing the centre, she gently placed the mighty sword Gram (Norse for wraith), which was crafted by the hand of Odin himself. And finally into the centre she placed the bone of Ullr, a bone of great power onto which the Norse god Ullr had carved many powerful spells.

After placing the final item Doideag flew back, throwing her arms up, and was lifted into the air by a strange glowing light of emerald green. Chanting in words that Danby could not make out, let alone understand, Doideag went into some kind of trance. Suddenly a transparent green wall emerged from the circle, which held inside it a giant tree, holding an entire island and with an equally impressive tree growing from the island's centre, which was holding what looked like a giant stately home cross castle both joined by two giant golden roads. Danby could not imagine anywhere this impressive, let alone think he would ever step foot into it.

Mother Nature said softly, "Danby, you will have to go. Doideag cannot hold it open much longer. You must find your own way back. Good luck and be careful child. I hope your father is safe and in this kingdom."

Danby looked at her and checked Mack was ready in his pocket. After saying thank you Danby stepped into the void.

Once stepping through, his ears popped and in an instant there was no evidence that the void ever existed.

It took Danby several hours just to reach the bottom of the great path. Looking up it seemed to be higher than any mountain that he had seen on television and made him wonder if they would ever reach its summit. Danby climbed the path for about three and a half hours before stopping dead and asking himself, "Could you really be that stupid?" and reaching into his pocket, gently took out Mack. "What do you think Mack? Hours wasted climbing this ruddy path when you could've had me there in minutes."

In an instant, there stood Pegasus, the mighty king of all winged horses. As Danby climbed on his back, he paused for a second before stating to Mack, "I like how you just slept and left me to climb this thing and never thought to offer to help me out." Mack just appeared to let out a massive horsey laugh and set off to transport his young friend to the summit of this magical realm.

On reaching the summit, the pair landed in a wooded area on the outskirts of Valhalla. There seemed to be no one about and the birds cheeped a very high beat tune, which seemed to get the blood boiling and your heart racing, filling you full of negative energy, and the strength to go into battle and die a good death.

Suddenly from the air, like a magnificent lightning bolt, and making an almighty thud on hitting the ground, a magnificent being holding on to a mighty hammer and as big as a house appeared from the dust. Danby jumped from out of the woodland and shouted to the mighty figure, "Excuse me? Sir? … Sir?

At which the figure turned. "Ha, ha. What are you? Are you here for the great hall of Valkyrie or Folkangr? The gentle pastures of Freyda perhaps?" and walked away holding his stomach and bellowing laughter.

"I am sorry sir. I am Danby and I need help," Danby shouted.

The mighty figure span round and angrily shouted at Danby, "Who are you to approach the mighty Thor? Son of

Odin and Frigg. Keeper of one of the nine realms of the Norse gods. Tell me, in which mighty battle did you fall, BOY? Now leave here," and walked away towards the mighty castle which stood in the centre of this land.

Danby backed up and put his arms around Mack's neck. "I am sorry to leave you in this shape Mack. I know you wanted to protect me, but we are in their realm and do not want to cause any trouble. We must respect people's ways in their own lands and I did not think I was in any real danger. I do think we will try down there though Mack. I do not like this place. I do not like this place at all."

Danby climbed onto Mack's back and the pair made their way down to the land below. There were several settlements bellow Valhalla. Danby decided to start his search on the easternmost settlement and make his way through them in a westerly direction. Upon reaching the first village he was greeted by a large gathering: men and women frolicking and getting extremely intoxicated, whilst fighting and singing songs of great battles. Danby instantly felt that this was not the place to find his father and left. He and Mack weaved across the Isle looking for Danby Senior. But settlement after settlement, they were greeted by the same sights and the same dreadful aroma of unwashed skin and stale alcohol. Danby's hopes of finding his father were forever diminishing.

There was one tiny village on the most westerly edge of the Isle. The pair circled round it for a while, looking for a safe secluded place to land. Upon spotting a small clearing, Danby pointed and Mack went in for a landing. Once on the ground, Danby noticed a very different atmosphere and a faint putrid smell which obviously radiated from the other villages and fortunately not this one. He rode in to the village on the back of Mack and soon came across a little cottage, all rundown and looking as if it had been empty for many, many years. Danby dismounted and went to take a look around. "I do not think we will find my father here, Mack," Danby said.

But then all of a sudden they heard movement, coming from inside. Danby transformed Mack into a giant gorilla once more. Mack was actually starting to feel quite comfortable in this guise. The pair walked toward the cottage cautiously and tried the rickety old door. The door seemed to be stuck but not locked. Danby asked Mack to have a go. So the mighty gorilla took hold of the door knob and with a gentle but firm tug, the whole door and frame came away. Mack just looked at the door and then at Danby and shrugged his shoulders. He placed the door and frame gently against the front of the house and then followed Danby through the gaping hole where it once used to reside.

Inside was a strange, sweet, exotic smell that seemed to take hold of the pair. The place looked derelict inside too, broken furniture and a hundred years of dust; but the pair did not mind or even notice as the sweet smell had carried their minds away to beautiful, carefree times. Within thirty seconds of the pair entering this rundown building, they just fell to the floor and slipped into a long dream. They just lay there in a dream state and the longer they were there, the weaker they would get. The dream state was meant to leave them in days of old. Happy days. With the illusion of wellbeing whilst your life slips slowly away.

About thirty-six hours had passed and a great light awakened them, to find that they had been chained tightly to the floor where they lay. Danby looked about confused and caught sight of Mack, who was also chained to the floor but in his original state. Danby was struggling to collect his thoughts but closed his eyes and concentrated on the mighty gorilla, which he was confident would have them free in no time at all. Danby laid there concentrating and waiting for the crash of chains once Mack had transformed. But instead the silence was broken by an old and stern voice: "It will not work."

CHAPTER XII

IS IT TRUE? HAVE THE DEATH BREATHERS LEFT?

Quickly focusing his attention towards the voice and taking a moment for his sight to completely return, Danby was shocked to see an old figure in front of him. Dressed in old tatty robes and with an old grey beard, which swept the floor as he walked.

"Who are you? Why are we chained?" Danby asked in a frightened and confused voice. "How long have we been here and what will not work?"

The figure walked across the room to a broken and woodworm-riddled old chair, and with a swipe of his arm, the old chair seemed to return to its original state. Like the day before it was ever sat on for the first time. The old man sat in the chair and put his hands together. He sat in silence just tapping his fingers together in deep thought until Danby broke the awkward silence. "Excuse me sir, but just who are you?"

"I will ask the questions young man. Have you no manners?" the old man said softly but firmly. "You are of man, yet you walk with the Schmee! How is this possible?" he continued.

"You know the Schmee?" Danby asked.

Standing up, the old man shouted, "I ASKED YOU A QUESTION!"

The air started to spin like a hurricane inside the cottage, dust and debris flying about everywhere. Danby was scared and just screamed out, "I am Danby and that is Mackschmee. Mother Nature sent me here to find my father."

The wind stopped. The dust and debris just fell to the floor. "I am sorry, but did you say Mother Nature? You expect me to believe that she would send a mere mortal into this realm to do her bidding? You must think me soft!"

Danby looked blankly at the old man and told the tale which had brought him to this moment. The old man started getting ready to leave the cottage after hearing Danby's tale. Once he had collected his things, he made straight for the door just saying, "You are very lucky I found you both. I only come to this cottage to harvest the parasitic fungus which had left you both incapacitated. I have to make enquiries. Upon my return and if I find you are lying, you will be returned to the state in which I found you."

As he made his way out the door Danby and Mack just lay there The old man had left them there for hours and Danby was starting to feel weak from thirst and hunger. He tried repeatedly to transform Mack but to no avail. Things were looking bleak for the pair when there was a deafening clunk and the chains just fell to the floor. In an instant, Mack was to his feet and standing as an eight-foot gorilla once more. Mack beat his chest ferociously and let out a mighty roar. "Calm yourself down Schmee. We have a lot to discuss."

The old man walked back through the door. Mack flew for the old man but half way towards him the old man just raised his finger and pointed. Mack just froze in mid-air, before falling to the floor in his original state. Danby gasped and asked in a shaky voice, "What are you going to do with us?"

The old man just stood in the doorway before suddenly opening his arms like he had a set of wings and saying, "Shhhhaaaaarrrrrrr, dinooook, tidum." And a blast of blue light flew from one end of the cottage and back again.

Once the light had finished and his eyesight came back, Danby was amazed to find everything in the cottage seemed brand new and immaculate.

"Please sit my friends? I am sorry for my behaviour but millennia in this realm would make a god learn to mistrust. Please sit?" the old man raised his arm, at which the table filled with a bountiful array of fine foods and drinks.

Danby ran straight to the table and started eating like a ravenous animal. "Slow down young man! We have plenty of time." The old man walked towards a frightened and confused Mack and told him, "Do not worry my faithful friend. I am sorry for my caution and am a friend of your mother Maschmee. Please?" and at that placed his hand flat on the floor. Mack cautiously climbed onto his hand. For the first time in his life he felt terror. He could not transform and was trapped in this delicate form in which a common moggie could take him out.

The old man sensed this and put Mack back down. In an instant Mack was in the form that he felt most comfortable in and you could see in Mack's face he was grateful. "You must excuse me my friend but a gorilla of your size is quite a daunting beast. Eat, my enormous friend, and we will talk." At that he clicked his fingers and a fire started in the old stone fireplace.

After eating Danby went and sat beside the old man who was staring into a crystal ball. "IS IT TRUE, IS IT, ARE THE DEATH BREATHERS ON MORTAL SOIL?" the old man shouted excitedly, and taking hold of Danby and shaking him vigorously asked, "IS IT TRUE?"

Danby spurted out, "Yes sir, yes it is true." The old man let go of him and walked in to the corner of the room. Pacing up and down whilst stroking his enormous white beard, he appeared to be in deep thought.

"Who are you?" Danby asked.

"I am sorry. How rude of me. My name is Merlin."

A wide-eyed Danby gasped. "THE Merlin?"

"You know of another?" Merlin asked.

"But how? Mother Nature told me what happened and said you have not been seen nor heard of since."

The old wizard just stood nodding his head for a short time before returning to his seat. Looking in to our hero's eyes Merlin started to explain. "Many years ago when the Death Breathers attacked I stayed right to the end and got as many of my Wickon friends to safety as I could. Once overpowered I created a portal to my friends, Odin and his beautiful wife

Frigg. I knew they would help and support me whilst I tried to put together a plan to defeat the Death Breathers. It has been futile though. The combined forces are proving to be too much for me to overpower. I have studied ancient and foreign magic but to no avail. Until now. I am sorry but the rise of the gods has presented me with a golden opportunity to reclaim the Wickons' lands. Now may I ask what has brought you strange pairing here once more and please leave nothing out?"

"Well, let me see. The gods have taken it upon themselves to de-evolve mankind, before we destroy the planet. Mystical beasts and animals of planet Earth fighting each other and destroying man's greatest achievements. An ancient bamboo, spreading and strangling the planet and somehow me and my father are tied into all of this through the Oshaki oak and the mighty Zeus himself. Oh! And the whole time being chased and attacked by all sorts of beasts and creatures, whilst searching for my father whom we believed to be dead for a time."

Taking a deep breath and looking over towards Mack, Danby asked, "Have I missed anything out?" Mack just shook his head and carried on nibbling at the abundance of fruit laid out in front of him. "Merlin please, could you in any shape or form, help me to find my father? I beg of you. Anything? I miss him so much. Loki was said to have brought him here, yet me and Mack have searched every inch of this horrible place and have yet to find any signs that he was even here. It looks like he was telling porkies. I do not know what to do."

Merlin looked into our young hero's eyes, and told him how Loki was there visiting his parents merely days ago .

"It is said he brought a new face with him to join the despised."

"The despised?" Danby asked.

"If it is your father of which they speak, we must find him immediately. There is no food grown in the wastelands or goods made. Only the strong survive as all they have to eat and keep them warm are the scraps discarded by the fallen. Those which have fallen in great battles along with those great warriors that lived a full but brutal life. Courage and brutality prevail here, and in their eyes only the strong are worthy of that survival. I am sorry child, but it is possible that your father might not have survived."

"No, my father's strong." And holding his head in his hands, sobbing, Danby asked Merlin once more for his help.

Merlin rose from his seat and walked towards the window deep in thought whilst stroking his white beard once again. "Charack. That is who we need. Charack. If anybody knows what has happened to your father, he will." Merlin headed quickly towards the door and as he went through it, he shouted to the pair. "It would probably be for the best if you two stay indoors, as it will serve no purpose if you are discovered."

Merlin was gone for several days, but left the pair a mighty feast. Upon his return, he found Danby and Mack playing cross morph. A favourite game of the Schmee, where Danby must think of the most ridiculous creature that he could imagine.

"Arrgggghhmmmm." Merlin cleared his throat to make our heroes aware of his return and quickly spun back round towards the door, and ushering someone in with his right arm, said, "Lay him there," pointing at the bed at the back of the room, that our pair could swear was not there a moment ago.

At this, a strange Quasimodo-looking figure backed through the doorway, holding in his arms what looked to be a body wrapped in a blanket.

"Quick. Over there on the bed," Merlin said to the stranger. The strange creature placed the bundle on the bed. "Quick boy water," shouted Merlin.

Danby ran to the table and brought back a goblet filled with life-giving water. On reaching the bed, Danby could plainly see it was his father laying there. With tears streaming, he climbed on to the bed and placed his father's head on his legs, slowly giving him sips of water. Danby stayed with him and tended his needs all night long. While tending to his father, Danby was introduced to Charack and thanked him for finding and saving Danby Senior. Charack had been dismissed to the lower levels and transformed into this hideous creature they saw before them by Odin himself, for what was, in Odin's own words, "Paying an inexcusable interest in his wife Frigg."

Danby fell asleep late the next morning and was awoken to Merlin and his father sat by the fire chatting. Danby ran into his father's arms.

"Dad. You are OK. Oh, I was so worried."

The pair just sat and cuddled for what seemed to Danby hours, but at that time he could not think of anywhere he would rather be. They sat through the night and made plans on how to get home.

"Now the Death Breathers are out of my kingdom, I must return. I am sorry my friends, but as you battle to save your home, so must I."

"But how do we get home?" Danby asked.

"I can take you back to my realm. You can take a system of magical tunnels back to where you need to be."

"I know the tunnels. I have spent time in them quite recently," Danby piped up.

Merlin took hold of them and explained. "So, you know how dangerous they can be. I am sorry, but on our return I have a safe room. Once we leave the confines of that, I am afraid you are on your own as I will have a giant hurdle of my own to get over."

Charack wished them well and made his exit. Danby, Mack and Danby Senior spent days helping Merlin gather what he needed and making plans for getting back home.

CHAPTER XIII

ON SUCH YOUNG SHOULDERS,
IT BREAKS MY HEART!

The day had arrived to make the journey home. Merlin was still running about doing his final checks, whilst the other three woke up and ate a hearty breakfast. "Just one more thing and we are ready," Merlin shouted and ran out of the cottage.

The three just sat and chatted for hours, during which Danby explained to his farther what had been going on since he had been taken and why these events had come to fruition. Danby Senior grabbed hold of his little boy and sat there sobbing, hugging him as tightly as he possibly could for what seemed like hours. His father could not imagine how sad and lonely his firstborn must have been to contemplate his own death. Especially wearing his father's helmet with the shard giving off such good feeling. His heart was breaking. Kissing Danby on the top of his helmet, he promised his son that he would never leave him again and would do all in his power to make things right. The burden Danby was carrying should have been given to someone much older, and Danby Senior was there to take that burden away from him.

Danby told his father, "It is OK now dad. You are back. We can get through this."

Danby Senior was the proudest parent alive to see how his son had grown up and at the confidence this young man was showing.

Suddenly Mack jumped up and Danby made it possible for him to resume his guise as the mighty gorilla. Listening intently, Danby asked, "What is that?" The thunderous sound of a thousand horses getting forever nearer.

Merlin burst through the door, pushing a large mirror as if it was just floating. Placing the mirror and making it stand up against the wall, Merlin spun round waving his arms about and chanting some incantation under his breath. A glorious blue veil covered the cottage, at which Merlin turned and informed the trio. "We had better get a move on. I had to erm…" He paused and then shouted out as if suddenly enlightened and nodding his head. "Borrow it. Yes. Borrow it. Now get everything together as we must go."

As they collected all the items Merlin had chosen to return with him, he placed candles and chanted once more in front of the mirror. As Merlin chanted, the mirror just seemed to melt away, revealing a large library hidden beneath the glass. "Come, come," Merlin beckoned.

Meanwhile the riders had arrived. Enormous, mighty men hacked at the blue light, trying to break in and shouting terrible threats toward Merlin. On stepping through the mirror Merlin conjured up what looked like a blue ball of plasma and fired it straight towards the mirror, exploding it into a million pieces. Looking puzzled, Danby was told, "We do not want them men to follow us. Believe me!"

Merlin instantly started looking about, pulling drawers out and throwing papers around. Suddenly the old wizard blurted out, "Ah. There you are!" And reaching into the back of a cupboard he produced a small golden box in the shape of a bee. Bringing it over and clearing the table, Merlin placed the box gently and with a smile on his face he unlocked and opened it. Laid there on a cushion of the reddest velvet was a small bee, lifeless and looking like it had been that way for over millennia.

While the three examined the strange bug, Merlin went searching once more on top of a round mirror hanging there in the centre of the wall. Upon stepping down off the files he had used to reach there, he produced a small, jewel-encrusted vial, which he opened and pulled open to show a needle as thin as a strand of hair and almost invisible to the eye, hanging down from the lid. Tapping it gently and forming the smallest of drips, Merlin proceeded to place the droplet on the tiny, sleeping bee's head. In a matter of moments it started to wake up and made its way towards the mirror where the life-giving vial was retrieved. Looking straight at Merlin it waited for him to open a tiny little porthole situated in the bottom centre of the mirror's frame. Half the size of a door's peep-hole, the little bee fitted perfectly.

Once the bee had entered the porthole, Merlin clapped and rubbed his hands together before rubbing them across the reflective part of the mirror and revealing exactly what our little airborne friend was seeing. Lingfeln had been destroyed. Merlin could not understand it. "For millennia they tried to take this land. Thousands dead! And for what? Why take this most beautiful of lands if all they wanted is to destroy it? This was such a beautiful land, yet now look at it."

Merlin flew into a rage and holding his arm out straight, a mighty looking staff flew out from the wall and straight into his hand. Putting his hand against the wall from where the staff had appeared to have come from. Danby Senior, with a look of wonderment on his face, asked, "How?"

Merlin just ignored his question and as he pointed his staff towards the wall, a doorway appeared. Throwing the doors open, Merlin marched through them in a mighty rage. Evil and twisted creatures raced towards him brandishing ancient weapons and throwing whatever heavy items the monsters could throw at him. Merlin and his staff just kept firing with rage. Creature after creature was evaporated in the beams emanating from his powerful staff whilst he threw others miles into the air with his free hand. Merlin was taking his home back and no power was going to stop him. Like a madman he fought and fought; drove after drove came at him, but with no effect. Mack tried to help Merlin, but a simple, split-second look from our enraged wizard kept him out of it except to protect Danby and his father.

BOOM, BOOM, BOOM. Three balls of fire hit the ground near our boys. Merlin span and quickly covered the other three in some kind of force field as three more bolts of destruction fell directly on top of them and sent Merlin flying into the air. Death Breathers, three of them. Danby had had enough. Whilst Merlin got back to his feet, our young hero imagined a sleek, razor-sharp phoenix. Made from pure diamonds and fast as a jet, Danby knew this creation could fly as he had seen it clearly in his mind's eye. Mack could not take off though. He would need something to jump off from. This could be problematic. Screaming with frustration, Mack jumped off anything he could, trying to gain height and catch a breeze under his magnificent wings, but crashed back to earth with every attempt. Seeing this, Merlin threw Mack high into the air, giving him the height he needed to stay there. Mack flew into the Death Breathers at sonic speeds, slicing through their hard exteriors bit by bit. This took them out of the equation as Mack was proving to be more than a match for them in this shape.

Meanwhile Merlin was heading towards the centre of town, trying to reach a mystical circle carved in the floor with a hole in the centre. On reaching his goal, Merlin immediately placed his staff into the small hole, which fitted the base of the staff perfectly. He shouted into the air: "Ianitor, iam, Ico, idcirco, evigilo, evince." At that a golden flash flew out from the staff, engulfing the land and seemingly clearing all evil from it. Mack was making easy work of the Death Breathers but was still relieved to see them thrown from this land along with all other evil.

The land had been destroyed over the years that Merlin was gone. By his own admission, he found it hard to recognize anything. At this, there were noises of shuffling and movement all around them. Danby returned Mack in to his favourite guise once again. Mack let out a mighty roar and thumped his chest violently before running towards the loudest of the noises.

Merlin froze him on the spot. "Patience, my mighty friend." And releasing him, continued, "I have a feeling that the noises you are hearing may be friendly. Let us just wait and see, shall we?"

Merlin cleared the debris from where they were stood, and after taking a deep breath proceeded to sit on the floor. Suddenly a mass of three-foot people engulfed Merlin, with cheers of jubilation echoing around this once again warm and enchanting land. Merlin got up and declared that he would give everyone a great feast and at that he started clearing room for an enormous rug, covered in the finest of foods and drink. "Relax and eat my friends and family. Tomorrow we start to rebuild."

Our three heroes got stuck in with the rest of the Wickons, but they were not all that hungry as Merlin had provided for them prior to their arrival. Well, that was except for Mack who seemed never to fill. Merlin pulled Danby to one side and introduced him to Sintar. "The three of us really must talk," he said, leading him back to his secret library which the mirror had brought them too and Merlin's safe room.

Once arriving in the library, Danby was shocked to see it had changed. The impressive library was now a grand sitting room, with three chairs sat in front of an open fire. In fact, the only thing not to have changed was the size of the room. "I do not understand!" Danby said with a confused look upon his face.

"It is simple." Merlin replied. "This is my home. All the rooms you have in your home are present here with a considerable amount more. Like you, I can only be in one room at a time! So I keep them all in here, calling up whichever room I need to be in, as you would walk through a door." Danby did not understand how he did it, but he agreed in principle. "Now, back to the business at hand. I have been discussing how to get you home and Sintar has just informed me that all the tunnels are guarded by Pan and his friends. There is one other tunnel that even the gods will not spend time in as it costs you dearly."

Danby looked at him, concerned at what this cost was if the gods themselves do their best to avoid it. "What could I possibly have to risk that the gods themselves will not risk to enter. What is in there?" Danby said, quite arrogantly.

"Simply time my child. Your time." Merlin replied. "In the tunnels of the Tempus Angelus, 'time angels' in your tongue. These ancient creatures milk you of your life force and feed upon it. This time will translate to your own upon your return.

84

You could spend a couple of days in these tunnels and on your return, weeks could have passed. They feed upon the missing time. You all have more than enough force to quite easily survive time in the tunnels but do not dawdle or deviate from the path. This could be very costly to you all indeed. I will get a message to Mother Nature that you will travel this path. Sintar will lead you to the entrance of the Tempus Angelus in the morning. But as for tonight, we would be honoured if you would be our guests."

Returning to Mack and his father, Danby informed the pair of the plan and the three of them spent the night enjoying Merlin and the Wickons' hospitality. The next morning they were awakened by Merlin and Sintar.

"I am sorry I cannot help you further, gentlemen, but I have been away many years and much work needs to be done. I hope you understand and wish you much luck. Be careful my friends and hopefully we will meet again in brighter times. I owe you so much. And because of that, please go safe in the knowledge that you will always find a place to lay your heads here in Lingfeln, also gratitude in the hearts of the Wickons and myself. Thank you!" And at that, Merlin picked up his tone and asked Mack to give his regards to his mother.

After finishing their goodbyes, the trio set off on their journey home, led by Sintar. "Is it far?" Danby Senior asked Sintar.

"Half a day's walk perhaps," he replied.

Spinning round, Danby Senior looked at Mack, about to suggest they could all travel on him somehow. The look he got from Mack answered the question without him having to even ask it!

CHAPTER XIV

IT'S GONNA BE A REET DODGY TIME GETTING AM, YER KNOW!

On reaching the entrance to the realm of the Tempus Angelus, Sintar suggested that the trio make camp and rest, as they were going to need all their strength to make it through the time-stealing caverns. "But we do not have anything to make camp with," Danby Senior added, not looking too keen at all at the prospect of sleeping on the floor.

"You forget where you are sir!" And with a few simple words from Sintar, a Bedouin-style camp just simply appeared, with tents, tapestries and the raging fire with food cooking.

Looking at Sintar, Danby Senior said, "I am going to enjoy travelling with you, little fella. Can you do this anywhere or just in these realms? You will have to teach me to do that," and with a satisfied look on his face, rubbing his hands together, Danby Senior made his way towards the fire and the beautiful-smelling food cooking on it.

"I am sorry sirs. I must leave you now and go help Merlin as we have a lot of work to do! I wish you well on your quest and hope you return from it victoriously! Good luck my new friends. We owe you everything and I hope our paths cross again. You ever need anything, all you need do is ask!" At that Sintar disappeared into the fire and the three of them were alone to find their own way.

"What the?" Danby Senior asked. With a stern and business-like look on his face he stormed over to Danby. "Right son, we need to talk. You told me what happens in this tunnel. I may not quite understand this, but it is obvious that we need to be in and out as quickly as we possibly can. We need to come up with something we can both ride in and out at supersonic speeds." Looking at Mack, he continued, "Well I do not know of any such creatures. You are from these places. Do you know of anything, Mack?"

Mack was still comfortable in his guise as a giant ape but realized that Danby's father was right. The mortals did not have a long enough lifespan for them to spend more time than they needed to in the tunnels. Looking at Danby and receiving nod of agreement, Mack pulled a twig off of one of the trees and sitting on the ground. He proceeded to draw the diamond phoenix that Danby had used to fight off the Death Breathers prior to travelling here.

"Of course," said Danby. "But I think I might imagine you a lighter body this time. Eh?"

Danby Senior just looked at them both with his eyebrows risen and said, "Sounds like a plan to me!" before summoning Danby and Mack over to eat.

After eating, Danby Senior took his young hero in his arms and the two fell asleep in each other's arms in front of the fire, with Mack on lookout. So much for not fancying sleeping on the floor.

The next morning the group left camp and made their way to the entrance. Closing his eyes, Danby concentrated on the mighty flying beast Mack had used to defeat the Death Breathers. This time though he was made from carbon fibre. Danby knew of this material as his father used it regularly in his Moto X career. Mack changed into a magnificent beast that looked like it belonged in a science fiction movie. Danby told Mack to have a practice flight before entering the tunnel, as they had no time to waste in there, the problem being that Mack could not take off from the ground. He would have to take flight like a glider once more. "Let us try again!" Danby imagined Mack the same, but with bigger and more powerful claws. "Can you claw your way up that rock face Mack?" he asked, pointing towards a totally vertical climb.

Mack started his ascent up the rock face and getting about thirty feet up he took off. Once in flight, Danby and his father struggled to keep track of him, he was travelling that fast.

"Wow. We will be in and out in no time!" Danby Senior said. "I suppose we had better make a move then." At which Danby called Mack back.

On his return, Danby and his father climbed on his back and hung on for dear life as Mack made his way into the home of the Tempus Angelus.

The tunnel was dark and damp, with shrieks and evil laughter echoing from wall to wall. A smell reminiscent of smoked kippers radiated from deep inside. This was not a nice place. They looked all around for the perfect spot from which to take flight. The shrieks were starting to get louder. They had better get a move on. About forty feet above them and a hundred feet in, they could see a small cave from which Mack could launch himself. Making his way towards it, Danby could see what can only be described as a swarm of evil and deadly-looking ghosts. "Quick. Look," Danby screamed whilst pointing towards their hosts.

Mack tried to climb as quickly as he could but speeding up slowed him down. Mack was just tearing rock from the wall. Mack stopped a split-second and took a deep breath before making an enormous leap as high as he could, bouncing off the wall into flight. The angels were upon them. Spreading his mighty wings he headed towards the ground, and with his breast catching the floor, Mack pulled up and gained height. By this time the angels were pulling and knocking into them to slow them down and steal the beautiful nectar of time from the three of them. Mack was going at some speed, though, and after a minute or two they were through the swarm. Mack headed to the roof of the cavern and with every descent he gained speed. Looking like a blur, the time angels struggled to get to them and within twenty hours they were arriving at the exit to the mortal's realm. The journey was not too bad at all and the three of them felt great.

"I do not know what the fuss was about!" Danby Senior said to his son whilst giving Mack a pat on the back for a job well done. The three of them walked through the exit.

Danby woke up to the sound of an engine beneath him and explosions all around. Where am I? Where are my dad and Mack? What happened? Where am I?" he screamed.

"Easy now boy. Tek a minute t' chill now… It'll be reet!" a strange voice said. The accent seemed familiar, though. At that, Danby's vision returned and in the corner was sat a man dressed in rags; with his feet up, he was playing on a small games console. "Be wiv y' in a sec son. Damned alien will not die." And he continued swaying left and right with the game, while biting his top lip.

Suddenly a succession of explosions rocked the van. The man jumped on Danby to protect him, and as they continued, the strange man lifted his head, smiled a not-a-care-in-the-world-type smile, looked Danby in the eye and with a wink said, "Soz 'bout that, ickle fella. Bit windy out there. You not got a clue who I is. Have ye?" Looking at him puzzled and not having a clue to what is going on, Danby just shook his head. "It's me. Yer favourite uncle." And taking Danby in his arms, giving him a quick hug and messing his hair, he continued, "It's me. Yer uncle Caine. You know… Yer ma's bruvva?"

With a look of realization Danby cried out, "Uncle Caine. What are you doing here? What is going on? Wh…"

"Chill fella. Chill." Caine stopped him in mid-sentence. "Look it's simples. Yer came out some shiny fing in Polokwane wiv yer dad and some ickle cute fing. Yer were out before yer hit the ground. We were sent t' get yer and tek yer safe t' meet our navy kiddies. Yer dad's in the CO's truck on the phone ter yer mam, and yer ickle friend's gone and climbed in yer pocket if yer av a look! Owt else? No? Then get yer 'ead back down, it's gonna be a long 'n' bumpy journey!" At that Caine just threw himself back into his seat and continued to kill aliens on his portable game.

Danby reached into his pocket and pulled out a sleeping Mack. In the hours spent in the tunnels, nearly three weeks had lapsed in his own realm. The three were robbed of this and never felt any of the effects of the feeding while in the realm of the time angels, but on entering their own realm time caught up, shutting their bodies down until time could even itself out!

Danby had been awake for several hours and his father had been back for quite some time now. "Divent worry ickle fella. We've gan through Pretoria and is well on't way to Cape Town. Nearly half way there kidda!" Caine piped up.

All of a sudden Caine's radio went off: "INCOMING AT TEN O'CLOCK. INCOMING." And all hell broke loose. There was a large convoy protecting our young hero as he was needed elsewhere. A dozen or so trucks full of the world's finest, a couple of American hemmt's carrying fuel and a few dozen Land Rovers and hummers, and all of them there just to make sure our young hero reached his destination.

Danby was feeling quite important when suddenly the truck was hit from the side by a giant rhino and sent flying on to its side. The passengers of the truck were tossed about like mother's washing in the machine. Danby Senior and Caine jumped on top of our hero and tried to shield him from injury as best they could. Once the truck came to rest, Caine dragged Danby and his father out to safety. There were dozens of mutated animals outside, ten times the size that they should be and intent on destroying the convoy. Anubis's hounds of hell were emerging from the ground, with a couple of Death Breathers thrown in for good measure. Danby quickly transformed Mack once again into the mighty ape he had come to know so well, but this time ten times bigger as to help against the mutated army: rhinos, gorillas, orang-utans, giant stag beetles, along with what looked like giant wolves with their eyes burning redder than hell itself.

"Come on, come on. MOVE!" Caine screamed at Danby and his father. "We have ter move. Mack? You stay ere an' watch our backs. I av ter get little fella out of 'ere. Divent let any one foller us," he screamed whilst collecting Danby and ushering him away from theatre.

Caine dragged them for miles, getting them as far away to safety as he could. A dozen or so of Caine's regiment had seen them making their escape and lagged a distance behind to try and ensure their safety. You could see the mighty battle for miles, with the soldiers being ordered to take the fight as far away from Johannesburg as was humanly possible. With a population of over three million, it would cause a real problem if the fighting reached the enormous city. Suddenly there was a roaring sound through the air. It was the Royal Air Force in their Euro fighters and silent death from above in the form of the Apache helicopters. There were explosions and gunfire everywhere. Danby was frightened for his friend Mack and tried to head back to the battle. Caine dragged him forwards. "Did yer not see the size ov yer mate? Made me bum nip! If a trusts anyone ter get out of a scrap, it's that big bugger," Caine shouted to Danby whilst running with him on his shoulder.

Mack at this time had left the heart of the fight and somehow linked up with Caine's men, clearing up the last of Danby's followers and making sure he travelled un-interrupted, before returning to his side. Caine's men found the trio hauled up in a small hut about five miles from where they were attacked. "Have you seen Mack?" Danby screamed.

"If you mean a giant ape approximately the size of me mam's house, then yes," came a voice. Stepping forwards and holding out his hand the soldier said, "Let me introduce myself. Staff Sergeant Roberts, at your service. So you are the nephew of Corporal Brown? This is some fine mess you have gotten yourself into young man. Your friend is hiding about a mile down the road in the tree line and trying his best not to draw attention to himself."

At that, Danby imagined Mack the same size as he was comfortable with, not knowing if it would work over such a distance and hoping that he had not placed his friend in danger by doing so, whilst Staff Sergeant Roberts continued, "There are still creatures patrolling and I think we should stay put until nightfall. Corporal Brown, could I have a word please?" And at that Staff Sergeant Roberts set off towards the door. Halfway through it he raised his weapon and, aiming it at something outside, he said firmly, "There is a much smaller version of your friend the gorilla heading straight for us! Do you know anything about this or do we class it as the enemy? Quickly, boy!"

At that Danby shot up and grabbed the gun which was pointing at his loyal friend. "No, no. Do not fire. It is OK. You were right, it is Mack."

Staff Sergeant Roberts gave Danby a firm look for touching his weapon and, storming out, he shouted firmly: "BROWN. NOW!"

As Caine left he just looked at Danby with a stupid smile on his face, shrugged his shoulders and continued to follow his superior officer.

CHAPTER XV

THAT DAMNED BAMBOO. WE ONLY HAVE FOUR DAY'S UNTIL THEY LEAVE!

When Lance Corporal Brown left the hut he spotted Staff Sergeant Roberts about thirty meters away, perched on a rock and smoking a cigarette. "Over here Brown," he shouted.

On reaching his superior who was pulling out his map, Caine was informed: "We are in trouble Brown. I was contacted on the radio just before the attack and they informed me that strange creatures are keeping our lads out of the sky and that ruddy bamboo stuff is blocking our path in nearly every direction. We have four days to reach a place called Klerksdorp. There is a chopper already on ground and we think it is possibly our best bet to get the boy and his father out of here."

Sharing the map, both men studied it. "It is about one hundred miles south of Johannesburg. South-southeast of the city are the Vaal Reef mines. We must make our way there for extraction to Cape Town. We have four days to reach the submarine HMS Astute before it has to disembark. Get a couple of hours' rest. It will be dark soon and we will move at twenty-hundred hours."

Caine, stood to attention, said, "yes sir." And after saluting, he made his way back to fill everyone else in.

Caine entered the hut and Danby was just sat silent in deep thought, stroking Mack in his original form, whilst the soldiers simply stared uneasily at what they did not understand. "Reet people, Listen up. This is what is gannin on. At twent......"

At that there was machine gun fire outside. "Stay 'ere, Danby son," Caine screamed as he ran outside.

A massive bellow rang all around them. "PLEASE MY FRIENDS, I BRING NEWS. I WISH YOU NO HARM."

Staff Sergeant Roberts screamed at his men to cease fire, not that it was having any effect anyway. Once the gunfire had stopped, the bellowing voice beckoned Danby outside. On leaving the hut, Danby was greeted by an enormous figure, dark as night and forty feet tall in traditional African dress.

"You must be Danby child?" the figure said as he made his way towards him. As he approached Danby, the figure started shrinking in to a more human size. "I am Cagn. One of the many gods that shaped this continent and an old friend of Mother Nature. That is why I am here, I have news. Pan has received word of your location and has set a trap for you in Cape Town, but unfortunately this is still your best option for returning home. You and your little friend there must stay clear of the sky as it is being watched. There are traps set for you everywhere. Mother Nature is setting to help you. Make swift my friends and good luck in the times to come!"

At that the mighty god raised his arms to the sides and in an instant he had transformed himself into a mighty blue crane and flew into the sunset as suddenly as he arrived.

"Well now. He divent tell us owt we didn't nae already. Muppet!" Caine said, quite condescendingly.

Twenty-hundred hours arrived and Staff Sergeant Roberts called his men in to give them instructions. "So you know your jobs. The radios have not worked since the attack. We do not know what is blocking them so stay sharp and in constant view of the man in front of you. Gentlemen, we are on our own. Right let's go!"

Heading back to where the convoy was attacked, our heroes set off, protected by a dozen or so soldiers. It did not take them long before they came across Pan's creatures as they seemed to be everywhere looking for Danby. Staff Sergeant Roberts was very good at what he did and managed to get Danby and his men back to the convoy without having to engage the enemy. There was debris everywhere and few vehicles were left in reasonable condition, even if overturned and smashed up somewhat. Staff Sergeant Roberts sent his men out on a reconnaissance of the area before venturing into the open to salvage vehicles. With both sides' dead littering the battle ground, our boys spent the next couple of hours trying to make two running vehicles out of the wreckage, when suddenly a friendly voice came screaming down the N1 in the direction of Johannesburg: "Smoggie! Smoggie!"

Looking up and listening to the voice behind him, Caine smiled a factor ten smile and spun round excitedly. Running towards the couple of dozen soldiers returning to the convoy in the full moon's glare, Caine screamed back, "Blade!" and meeting in the middle the men hugged a manly hug.

Pushing each other off Caine said to the big battle-worn Barbadian, "Where yer been man? Yer missed it! Sleepin is it? You'll neva mek a soldja," and flinging his arm round his large friend said, "Come meet our Elen's fella and their sprog Danby."

As Caine strolled back to introduce his family to his good friend, Staff Sergeant Roberts cut them off and reminded them in a firm voice, "We do not have time for this gentlemen. Lance Corporal Barrow, report please."

Standing to attention, Lance Corporal Barrow replied, "Yes sir. Once we lost sight of your escort the radios went dead sir. A majority of the creatures disbursed, presumed searching for you sir! Myself and the international survivors you see before you now took it upon ourselves to hunt down and destroy all of the creatures heading down the road to a massively populated area sir! Johannesburg sir! On deeming it secure sir, we returned here sir!" He spoke in a very condescending tone.

With an annoyed look on his face, his superior told him to stand down.

Returning to their tomfoolery, Caine and his friend continued on their journey toward Danby and his father. "Danby an' Danby's dad. This is me good mucka Blade. His real name's Ondre but 'e finks he's that Wesley Snipes bloke."

Slapping him in the stomach, Caine added, "Not a bad bloke though!"

Ondre made his way towards Danby and his father with absolutely no emotion on his face. Holding his hand out he said, "So... You two brought me here for this?" And turning his attentions toward Caine, he added whilst nodding his head, "Well I suppose it is not as bad as watching Middlesbrough play football!" and laughed.

Caine slapped him around the back of the head whilst saying, "Cheeky bugger!"

As the night drew on, the collected group of soldiers from around the world worked tirelessly to salvage whatever means of transportation they could. Once finished Staff Sergeant Roberts called the sentries back and brought everybody up to speed. "Head count please. Now, we have one old five toner, one Rover and a couple of humyees, two operational and mounted fifty cals and whatever munitions you lot are carrying!"

At that the head count came back: "Forty-three men including the civilians, sir."

Staff Sergeant Roberts continued. "It is oh-two twenty-three now. We have until eleven-hundred hours Friday before the transport disembarks. This gives us less than four days to get there. Now gentlemen, we have a problem. We do not have enough transport for everyone. I therefore apologize as we only need our fittest men on this mission if we are to succeed. The injured and whoever is not one hundred per cent fit are to be the first to volunteer to stay behind. We are ordered not to travel through any densely populated areas, so our only other option is to go around." Getting out his map once again and studying it in the headlights of the old five-ton troop carrier, he continued. "Once leaving here we head southeast for Witbank, if we head down to Kroonstad, we should hopefully pick up the mines on the way! Make sure everybody knows what they are doing, Corporal Brown, and be ready to go in ten."

Caine and his pal Ondre did as they were instructed and got everything ready for their departure. The much smaller convoy set off in blackout drive: Staff Sergeant Roberts in a hummer leading, the five ton with as many as it could carry, Caine, Ondre, Danby Senior, Danby and Lance Corporal Keith 'Slick' Nichols following in the second hummer, with the Land Rover following at the rear. Slick was a quiet and powerful-looking man, also from the suburbs of Middlesbrough, always up for a good set too and seldom sat still. "Good Boro stock," as Caine would say.

They had been driving for about half an hour or so and everything was going well, when they spotted the bamboo for the first time and could swear that you could physically see it growing.

This was foretold you know?" said Ondre, staring out of the window at the creeping plant.

"Shut. Up. You. Muppet!" Slick added from the hammock he was sat in, manning the fifty cal and looking at Ondre as if he was stupid. "Ruddy religion, the cause of all evil. Don't want any of that in 'ere. I mean, look what's goin' on!" And shaking his head, he just returned to watching the skies.

After an awkward few seconds of silence. "Reet, what ya wafflin?" Asked Caine with an uninterested look on his face.

His attention still on the magical bamboo, Ondre continued: "In the book of Isaiah, the first thirty-nine chapters are believed to be written by Isaiah's own hand. These chapters warn us of upsetting God, and his wrath if we do so. One chapter reads something like: the world a-mourns and withers. Fouled by its inhabitants, the curse will devour the Earth and those who live upon it!" Turning to Caine and suggesting with his hand that he took a look out the window, Ondre continued, "Well?" The vehicle went quiet and they just continued on their way.

Their journey had been quite uneventful when they came across a sign for Vaal Reef mines. There was nothing to see for miles but every now and again the occasional screech of a Death Breather in the distance reminded them how much danger they were still in. Upon reaching the mine, they found no one was there. Staff Sergeant Roberts pulled the lead vehicle up and stepped immediately out of it, quietly ordering everyone to get out of the vehicles. Having a quick look around, he quickly spotted a little watch hut about a hundred meters or so away from them. He shouted Caine over and pointing towards the hut he gave Corporal Brown his orders. "You, Nicholson and Barrow, take the kid and his dad and lay low over there in that hut until we have established contact. Do not, I repeat, do not give your position away at any costs. We were sent here to get your family home... And that is just what we are going to do! Am I understood?" At that he turned to Danby and ruffling his hair said. "It will be OK, lad. Got some of the Queen's finest watching that rear of yours." And nodding his head to represent some of the others behind him, continued, "Oh, and with a selected few, handpicked from around the world. So be brave and be quiet as we have it covered... We will get you home." Danby Senior was starting to feel more and more useless and unneeded as time went on.

It was less than half an hour before someone came to retrieve them. "Captain Shannon Thompson at your service, I hear you are in need of a lift?" And at that, the beautiful helicopter pilot walked Into the cabin where our heroes were laid low.

Wide-eyed and open-mouthed, Caine spluttered "Did yer see that?" And running out of the hut to catch her up, he continued, "I fink one is in love."

As the rest left the hut to follow, there were shrieks of the Death Breathers getting closer, and quickly too. "Hurry, the chopper's hid in the mines. I left some of your men dragging it out." And dragging at our young hero, she screamed, "Come on... Do you not want to get out of here?"

The mines were about five minutes away and the soldiers had gotten the chopper out of the mine and were preparing to get it started. On arriving at the mighty helicopter, Captain Thompson took her seat while the rest of them climbed into the back. Captain Thompson took off immediately and had just set off in the course of Cape Town when there were at least three Death Breathers chasing them and getting closer by the second. Suddenly blue fireballs went hurtling past them as the Death Breathers were upon them. Captain Thompson took evasive manoeuvres but the Death Breathers were just too agile. "I cannot shake them. We must land before they knock us out the sky."

"TWO MINUTES?" Danby cried, "Just two more minutes? Open the rear hatch," he asked one of the soldiers, who just looked about confused.

"DO IT!" Caine screamed. At that the soldier jumped up and grabbed the switch that opened the back up.

Meanwhile, Captain Thompson was having to pull off some rather magnificent moves to avoid the Death Breathers, who were intent on knocking the helicopter straight out of the air. "Whatever it is you are thinking of doing, you better make it now!" As she said this, one of the Death Breathers had gotten in front of them and was making his way straight for them.

Once the rear hatch was half open, Danby took Mack from out of his pocket and threw him out. Closing his eyes Danby imagined the biggest, most evil dragon he could. Suddenly this huge dragon had evened the odds somehow. Flying in front of the chopper, Mack took his first victim in his enormous talons, and holding him there, he headed angrily for the other two that were in pursuit. While Mack battled with the Death Breathers, Captain Thompson took this time to make their escape.

CHAPTER XVI

THAT WAS FAR TOO EASY!

It had been much easier than anyone had anticipated to reach Cape Town so far. The odd Death Breather, but Mack seemed to be more than a match for them. They had had it good so far and they had not seen any sign of the enemy for at least twenty minutes. Ondre looked at Caine with a smug smile on his face, and undoing his seat belt he got up and made his way to the cockpit. Squatting down next to Captain Thompson, he commented, "This is some size bus. My kinda ride!" and nodding his head whilst looking around aimlessly, he added, "You like big men too then, sweetheart?"

A few silent seconds passed, and then Captain Thompson replied sharply: "This is a Sikorsky CH-53E Super Stallion. This particular vessel is used to deploy marines from USS Bataan and was graciously loaned to us by their captain for this mission only. I have handled much bigger than this." And turning to look Ondre straight in the eye, she continued, "SWEETHEART! And have crashed bigger than you! So if you would like to return to your seat, a stewardess will be by shortly and if you are a good boy, you might get a packet of peanuts. Have a safe flight and goodbye."

Everyone in the back of the mighty vessel were laughing and jeering at Ondre as Captain Thompson had flicked the intercom on as soon as she noticed him entering the cockpit. Obviously, he was not the first soldier to hit on this particularly beautiful brunette. Getting back in to his seat and taking the ribbing on the chin, he simply looked at Caine and told him, "Piss off," as he re buckled his seat belt.

Just as he clicked his belt on, a sudden BOOM came from the rear of the chopper. Suddenly: "Death Breathers, dozens of them. They have taken out the rudder. Prepare for crash landing. I repeat. Prepare for crash landing!" came Captain Thompson's voice over the internal intercom. She was having a nightmare to keep the mighty Sikorsky in the air , but It was starting to spin faster and faster, Captain Thompson was fighting with the joystick and pedals, but it was no use. They were heading for the ground, never mind how hard she tried. Mack had seen them hit and was fighting off as many Death Breathers as he could to keep them from reaching the chopper. It was to no avail though, there were just too many of them. Mack was being overpowered and there was nothing anyone could do. Mack's screams could be heard for miles. Blood-curdling screams!

Danby's father had managed to get Danby out of his seat and buckled in with him before the mighty helicopter hit the ground. Thrown about in his seat with his father, but relatively unhurt, Danby ran straight through the back of the Sikorsky where the door had twisted and had left enough room for him to get out. With tears streaming down his face, Danby looked to the skies for his best friend Mack, just in time to see him brought to ground by hoards of the evil Death Breathers. Slick grabbed him from behind; picking him up, and with the Death Breathers turning their attentions towards them, he made his way as far from the helicopter as possible. "I need to get you to cover, wee man. There is nothing you can do for your friend now."

Kicking and screaming, Danby had no choice but to go with him. Danby Senior was never far from his side and was feeling lower than ever on seeing his boy in this state.

Grabbing Caine's firearm, Danby Senior turned and fired a full magazine towards the direction of the Death Breathers, shouting, "WHY...WHY...? He is just a boy!" and falling to his knees and, heartbroken, he continued quietly to the ground, "He is my boy."

Caine grabbed Danby senior and dragged him all the way to cover. Luckily they never had to run far, before they found a small derelict house. Covered in sand over time, it was almost invisible. Eight or nine soldiers stayed outside and camouflaged themselves as lookouts. Slick had to keep Danby quiet as he was still wanting to go and find Mack. On seeing Mack's mighty frame hitting the ground, Danby had imagined him as a tiny little mouse, hoping that he could escape down a crevice or crawl under something, anything. Danby was worried and scared for both him and the rest of them.

"Any casualties?" Staff Sergeant Roberts asked everyone.

"That French kiddie and Mason never got oot the chopper sir, few cuts an' bruises sir, now't serious though!" Caine answered him whilst looking about to see if he was right.

"Good, let us have a look where we are!" Staff Sergeant Roberts replied. As he took out his map, Captain Thompson joined the pair and told him, "We are about forty miles north of Cape Town," and pointing on the map, added, "Here. I saw a railway track just west of here as we were coming down. That has to be it marked there; if we follow it into Cape Town, it should lead us straight into Victoria and Albert Docks, where we are meant to rendezvous with Captain Sheard of the HMS Astute. If we come off them behind these gardens it should only be half a mile or so to the extraction co-ordinates."

Meanwhile, at the back of the hut, Danby Senior was not looking to good and Danby had noticed this. Pushing Slick off and making his way towards him, Danby asked, "Are you OK Dad?"

His father looked into his eyes and said, "You must be so ashamed, son. A father that cannot protect his family, I am so, so sorry," before burying his head back into his knees.

Caine was watching this as he finished up with Staff Sergeant Roberts and on being dismissed, he made his way straight towards Danby Senior and dragged him to his feet by his arm, and peering straight into his eyes, told him. "Gan an' grow a pair. Yer lad needs yer ter stay strong man. Not ter fall ter bits like this. Suck it up and ger a grip, War showin' us up man!"

At that, Private Burns walked in and informed Staff Sergeant Roberts that the enemy had left in a south westerly direction. "I would love to know what they are up to!" Staff Sergeant Roberts replied, whilst looking to the skies through the window.

On hearing this news, Danby ran straight out the door towards were his best friend Mack had fallen. With tears streaming down his face, he cried out to his friend, over and over again. Danby reached the area which he had seen Mack hit the ground, moments before Caine, Slick, Ondre and his father, who was starting to bring himself round after Caine's strict words. The five of them started to search the area very carefully, as not to step on our little friend.

After ten minutes or so of searching, Slick spotted a small amount of blood near a large rock. Upon investigating a small hole under it, Slick was heartbroken to find Danby's little friend, who had given his all to keep them safe in the skies, hanging onto life by a thread. Taking his shirt off, Slick dug around the hole to give him room to lift Mack out safely and without causing any further damage. Wrapping him up gently in his shirt and wiping the blood from our little hero, Slick carried him over to Danby, with a lump in his throat and unable to speak.

Danby looked over and saw the giant of a man fighting to hold back tears, and knew instantly that it was bad. He ran towards Slick, who just fell to his knees, and screamed "MACK......NO!

He took his friend gently from Slick and sat cuddling him for a good ten minutes. "Mack... Please Mack. I do not know what to do Mack... Please Mack, do not die?" Danby whispered to his brave friend.

His father sat beside Danby and put his arm around him. "I am so sorry son, but we have to go."

Danby got up, never taking his eyes off of Mack and walked off, cradling him gently, like a new born baby. On returning to the hut, the others were packed up and ready to leave. Walking towards Danby and stroking Mack's head gently, Staff Sergeant Roberts told him, "I am sorry son. We have waited as long as we could and we must leave."

It took them no more than an hour to reach the tracks and they came onto them about twenty miles north of Worcester. For the first time, they had come across the bamboo and had to change course to go around it. Towns and villages had just been swallowed up by this ancient plant. Travelling in darkness and resting in daylight, our heroes were getting hungry. It hit morning and there was still over twenty-four hours left to get the kid and his sick pet to the boat.

Mack was in a bad way and just kept slipping in and out of consciousness. Danby was terrified that he was going to lose him. He remembered from a film that the Wolverine has great healing powers. Closing his eyes and wishing harder than he had ever done before, Danby was devastated to see Mack laid there in his own form still and as lethargic as ever.

"He needs help!" Danby pleaded to anyone who would listen. "We have to go now! He needs help!"

At this the sun was getting higher and they were still just short of thirty miles from their destination. Captain Thompson called everyone out from their shelter. "It is less than thirty miles to our extraction point, gentlemen and I do not think our little friend will survive without treatment." Looking towards the south, she pointed: "You see those dark clouds over there? Well that is where we need to be and somehow I get the feeling that they, gentlemen, are not clouds. The decision is yours to make! I myself feel that none of us would be here now if it was not for his bravery and am damned if I am going to sit back without giving him a fighting chance! I vote we go now and get the little fella some help, any objections?

The soldiers looked around at each other, before Slick cocked his weapon and said, "I am getting to feel a bit stiff like. Could do with the exercise," and set off back down the lines towards the city. One at a time the rest followed and it did not take long before they could see clearly what it was that filled the skies above with darkness.

"Ruddy Hell," Ondre said, eyes wide open and catching flies, "dragons, bloody thousands of them!"

Spreading out, everybody kept close to the shrubbery on their way into town. Before long, they came across the ancient bamboo blocking their way. "Can we not cut through it?" Danby asked his father.

"I do not think so son. It looks too dense and would probably take us days," he replied.

Looking at his father and with his eyes wide open, he shrieked, "NO! WE CAN'T, WHAT ABOUT MACK?"

"To me," came a voice from in front of them. Staff Sergeant Roberts had beckoned his men to him and was asking for suggestions. With no realistic plan to speak of, he informed them, "Well, there is only one solution then." And looking over his shoulder, he added, "We must go around it."

Reaching in to his thigh pocket, Staff Sergeant Roberts beckoned everybody closer to study the map and gave out his orders. "Right we are here, near the Pinelands. We are going to head for the observatory and reassemble there. On reaching the observatory, we will reassess the situation on having had a closer look. Thompson, you can come with us. Slick, Dre, Smoggie, you are with me!" Standing up and whistling for everyone's attention he instructed the others: "Listen up. The rest of you, split into groups of five. Be careful and for Christ's sake, stay away from open spaces, there are too many places for an ambush, for my liking... I repeat, we will head for the observatory and will meet up there. Try and keep in sight of the other groups and we will reassess the situation once we have had a closer look. Good luck and stay safe, gentlemen." At that, he picked his weapon up and set off in the direction of the observatory, ushering our hero and his bodyguards to follow.

The observatory was a couple of hours from their position and they were finding it hard to keep up the pace, as the sun was beating down with all it had to offer. On the way, Danby looked for any signs of life, as he had been travelling across this magnificent country for a couple of days now and was still to come across a single human being, aside from the group he was travelling alongside.

Once reaching the observatory, they stayed back and took stock of the situation. Staff Sergeant Roberts sent two teams in to have a look around and with a few sentries scattered strategically between them. The radios were still not working and he felt this was the safest and quickest way to ensure his men's safety. The teams surrounded the building before sending three men in to check it was safe. Within seconds, you could hear machine gunfire and loud screams.

"Captain Thompson, Smoggie, Slick, Dre. Keep the package safe!" Staff Sergeant Roberts screamed, as he took off towards the observatory, waving the rest of the troops to join him.

Suddenly, from every direction, Anubis's hounds were everywhere. As Danby and his bodyguards watched, there was the sound of heavy breathing all around them. "I don't see anything. Do you?" Captain Thompson quietly asked Caine.

"No," he replied. "But I think we should move."

Cautiously getting up, they started to move. As Dre held back to watch their retreat, a mighty beast became visible, from behind foliage. Opening fire, two more became visible. "MOVE, MOVE, MOVE," he screamed.

With Slick and Caine dropping back to help their friend, Captain Thompson tried to navigate Danby and his father through the ensuing battle and into the observatory. There was a battle raging inside, but it was sure to be a safer bet than staying out in the open.

"Secure the observatory!" Staff Sergeant Roberts instructed his men. The men inside were just clearing up the last of the mighty foes. These beasts took some wiping out. As the men made their way inside, Captain Thompson could see that Caine, Slick and Ondre were pinned down by the mighty foe. Grabbing a weapon and making her way outside, she told an unlucky couple of soldiers, "With me!" and kicked the doors open.

Firing at anything that moved, she and the two soldiers, made their way towards the three friends and trying to clear a safe path, took position to give covering fire. "Corporal Brown. To me," she shouted, instructing him to make his escape. Laying down covering fire and managing to hold the beasts back somewhat, Captain Thompson instructed them to make straight for the observatory. Fighting their way back to cover, Captain Thompson was pinned down, two mighty beasts circling her and cutting off her escape.

Suddenly, as Caine and his men tried to reach them, a third beast came from nowhere and with a lightning fast attack, carried Lance Corporal Ramirez off with it. More and more of the beasts kept arriving. Several men by this time had been overpowered and the ranks were getting weaker. Smashing the windows, the men had been concentrating their fire on getting Captain Thompson and her colleague back to safety, but with more and more beasts arriving, this was proving futile.

Staff Sergeant Roberts was trying in vain to radio for back-up, but the radios were still being blocked. "Damn it. We do not have a chance," he said to himself.

Suddenly, pinpoint explosions started to hit the beasts. Staff Sergeant Roberts was relieved that the air force had found them. "Quickly, get everyone inside," he instructed his men. At this, the men not covering the windows, made their way to the exterior of the building and gave covering fire until everyone was inside. "Captain Thompson. Good to have you back! I do not know whose air force that is, but they sure saved our behinds!" Staff Sergeant Roberts claimed.

Looking confused, Captain Thompson asked him, "What air force? There was no air force. Look," and dragging him to the window, pointed up into the sky. "They're not air force." Staff Sergeant Roberts was amazed by what he saw.

Two giant dragons, one red and sleek, with enormous, razor-sharp talons and scales that looked like they would cut through you like butter. The other was pretty much as you would imagine a dragon. In fact, it looked exactly the same as the dragons that had saved Danby and Mack from the Death Breathers earlier. Overpowered and losing strength, the hounds started to disperse as quickly as they had arrived. At this, the two mighty beasts landed. "Keep your weapons on them," Staff Sergeant Roberts ordered.

"No. It is OK. They are on our side, they want to help us!" Danby screamed, before running out the door. "Please? Please? Mack has been hurt. You have to help him? Please?" and showing them his injured companion. The red dragon replied to this in a language Danby could not understand.

"I am sorry, young Danby. Said the other dragon in a thick Irish accent. One should introduce oneself. I am O'Shea, Ruler of the Irish Dragon clan. And my mighty companion is Barack, ruler of the fierce Indian Red breasted clan. I am sorry, but Barack only speaks Hindi, so one must translate. What my mighty companion was trying to tell you is that we do not have the power to save Mackschmee. I do not know if anyone has. I really am sorry."

At that, Barack turned towards the direction of the Victoria and Albert waterfront, all agitated. "The Death Breathers are preparing to attack your fleet. We are massively overpowered and must return now. Have courage little one and hope Mother Nature and her friends reach the fleet soon!" O'Shea translated as the pair prepared to take back to flight. Once airborne, Danby could hear O'Shea wishing them luck and making a strange noise, which to Danby sounded like he was actually getting excited.

"Quick. Everybody back in the building," Staff Sergeant Roberts ordered.

Everyone did as ordered and once inside, Staff Sergeant Roberts went back to his map and placing it on Corporal Butterfields back, pointed and told everyone, "Right people, we are here and we need to reach the rendezvous point here, as soon as humanly possible. I sugges…"

And at that he was cut short by Danby Senior, "Sorry but everybody needs to see this!" and returned to Danby two floors up; the rest followed.

On reaching the canteen, they found Danby and his father staring intently out of the window. Looking across towards the waterfront, everybody was amazed with the sight that greeted them. The ocean was full of hundreds of military warships, from the furthest reaches of the globe and with hundreds of Barack and O'Shea's dragons circling the skies; it was an amazing sight that kept them all in silence, until a voice broke it. "Right people. We have to get to them ships, and fast."

Looking over and spotting a leaflet holder, Staff Sergeant Roberts approached it and continued on to find a bunch of street maps of Cape Town. Handing them out, he gave his orders. "Right people, this is the plan. We will leave via the rear and make our way onto Barrington Road. We will follow this onto Station Road and taking a left onto lower Maine Road. Following this to its end, we will take a left onto Malta Road, which turns into Albert Road, just beyond the roundabout. Lower Church Street, Nelson Mandela Blvd and finally onto South Arm Road. Any problems, we will meet up in the Graduate School of Business on the other side of the dock." Looking around the room, he asked, "Right, any questions? No. Good. We leave in fifteen!"

CHAPTER XVII

I AM SORRY SON. IT LOOKS LIKE
WE ARE DONE FOR!

The fifteen minutes was up and everyone made their way out the back door, as Staff Sergeant Roberts sent them out one at a time, instructing them to use the station road overpass for cover as there was an overwhelming shriek, filling the hot, dry afternoon and a darkness consuming Cape Town. The Death Breathers were starting to arrive in droves. Keeping their distance from each other, our hero and the thirty or so soldiers were all feeling on edge and wondering how they were going to get to the extraction point. Explosions started to echo everywhere. Dragon fighting dragon, with the world's military trying to keep the coast clear; and all for one small boy from the Boro.

They used the cover of the Station Road overpass for as long as possible, before having to scrap their plan as it soon became apparent that it was every man for himself. With thousands of Death Breathers keeping O'Shea and Barack's dragons busy, it was now safe for the Hounds of Hell, and whatever other creature were lurking, to march safely through the city and search for our young hero unhindered.

Ground forces had been deployed, but could not advance due to the Death Breathers: hundreds of British and American Apaches, German Tigers, Russian MI-28s and KA-50s, Indian Bangalore, etc. Every nation had a presence in this South African city and all at once. It was a magnificent sight but the most terrifying time that anybody involved had ever experienced: ships being sunk, dragons and machines falling out the skies in droves and the ground shaking with the explosions everywhere. Things were looking more and more impossible.

Danby and his father were being dragged through the streets and Danby Senior had just received the world's fastest master class in weaponry. Caine, Ondre, Slick and Captain Thompson had pulled Danby and his father from under the overpass once the fighting started. The four of them thought it would be safer to use the cover of the city as it had been compromised and the roads were, in places, just too much in the open. Fierce battles were going on all around them, with building exploding and falling down all over the city. Caine was starting to think that he was not going to be able to get his young nephew and brother-in-law to safety. All he could think of was his sister, sat at home and not knowing where her son and husband were or if they were safe.

The international forces were starting to gain ground, be it only a matter of feet at a time, getting the odd soldier through and more and more fire from the mighty ships getting to its target. The Death Breathers just kept coming, though. Suddenly, high above their heads, the screech of a thousand eagles and something almost completely blocking the light from beating down. The air cooled to a much more comfortable temperature. The skies were full and it was getting more and more difficult to work out who was who.

The dark cloud started to break up and Danby was relieved to tell the others, "It is Tyra and her army of griffons. Mother Nature will not be far behind her I hope!"

"So, they are on our side?" Slick asked. Danby just nodded and Slick released a massive sigh of relief.

Danby and the others watched as Tyra's army joined the battle, but no one could see who was involved in this ferocious battle The ships were now rendered almost inert at this moment and were now firing for defensive purposes only. A large group of Tyra's soldiers had peeled off and were helping the ground troops to take control of the city. Anubis's hounds and strange creatures everywhere, the griffons showed that they were as formidable foe on the ground as they were in the air.

Things were starting to get dire for the fleet. Sea serpents and a multitude of mutated sea creatures were joining the battle, which spread out for miles. This was starting to look like the end for the planet. Mighty ships being torn apart and sunk from air and sea, more and more creatures entering the city, causing destruction in their wake and with machine and creature alike falling from the skies in their droves, it certainly did not look good for us as a race.

Trapped in the centre of the city, our group made their way towards a small Bakalla (a small grocery store, usually open-fronted). Needing food and drink, the six of them took their fill. "We have to go. Mack's not doing too well. He needs a doctor," Danby told the other five.

Captain Thompson made her way over to Danby and reached out for him to pass her his injured friend. "Here let me take him for a while. You must be getting tired?" She said to him, but Danby was having none of it.

"No. It's my fault. We must hurry! I do not think he has long left," he told the beautiful helicopter pilot, with tears running down his face. At this time, Danby would switch places with his friend in a heartbeat.

Taking a gentle look at Mack and ruffling Danby's hair, Caine told the group, "Well it looks like the footy's gonna be off and a ain't got nowt else ter do! Anyone up for a row?" and at that he proceeded to make his way back outside. Quickly filling their pockets on the way out, the rest followed. "Reet, this is the plan. We run ter the rendezvous and don't stop for owt. Shoot owt that moves and no one get killed. Any questions?"

Slick put his hand up in the air. "Do yer fink there's any bevvy on them there ships?" he asked. The others just shook their heads and moved out. "What? Just a thought," he added.

Danby, his father and their escort set off at double pace and it was not long before they came across the enemy: a pack of wolves, as big as horses and glowing red eyes that gave you a window into hell itself. "Not again," Ondre said as he ushered the group into a doorway.

Taking cover behind a couple of child's rides, the group opened fire. These mighty beasts were not easy to destroy, though. Round after round was put into them before they would fall. Slick fired grenades but there were just too many of them. More and more beasts were congregating on their position and ammunition was running dangerously low. "I am sorry kidda. I'm not sure if were gonna make it. We need a miracle!"

At that, one of Anubis's hounds appeared as if from nowhere and lunged straight for our hero. Taking the butt of his rifle, Ondre jumped in front of our young hero and hit the hound as hard as was humanly possible. At this the hound crashed straight into the mighty Barbadian. Crushing him against the wall, immediately the evil and unremorseful hound got back to his feet. Slick, full of rage, placed himself between the creature and Danby and emptied what was left of his magazine into it. Running out of bullets he reached for his knife, which was always strapped to his leg, and in a blind rage lunged at the creature, punching and slashing at it until it breathed no more.

Quickly making his way to his friend Ondre, while the others did their best to hold off their attackers, Slick was shocked to see Ondre's left arm had been broken and part of his humorous was protruding through the skin, between his bicep and tricep.

"Go help. I will be OK. Go!" Ondre told Slick as he laid there trying to stay conscious. Picking Ondre's weapon up and turning to help his companions, Slick was gutted to see a whole array of creatures moving in on them and simply thought to himself, "CRAP!"

Suddenly, about a dozen griffons which had spotted the creatures' movements and followed to see what was going on, flew directly into their enemies and fought alongside them until the threat was beaten into retreat. Slick and the others dropped back at this to go and tend to Ondre. "Blade son, you OK? Yer lookin a bit pale there marra," Slick asked him.

Ondre just closed his eyes and with a smile shook his head gently.

Suddenly there was an explosion behind them and the griffons took back to the skies, leaving three of their companions laying there without life. "Quickly, get him to his feet. We do not have far to go now but we must keep moving... In case anyone has forgotten, there are things trying to eat us everywhere. So come on!" Captain Thompson screamed at the soldiers, whilst trying to pull Ondre to his feet.

Danby shot up from the corner in which he had been hiding and keeping Mack from further harm and from which his father never left his side. "She's right and we must get Mack treatment if he is to survive," Danby Senior added after seeing how keen his son was to get a move on.

"He is right, let's do one. Quick, just strap me up," Ondre said, gritting his teeth and waiting for the pain to begin.

"I am so sorry my friend, we have no pain killers," Slick informed his colleague as he proceeded to strap up his arm. Dre give out a loud grunt before falling to his knees. After a few seconds he held out his hand to be helped back to his feet and just simply grabbed his weapon back from Slick and set off in the direction they were headed.

Captain Thompson kept Danby and his father close as the other three circled them with their eyes peeled for more creatures. Before long, they had started to come across what was left of the mighty ground force. Taking over sixty per cent casualties, these brave men and women continued to battle bravely. "Have you seen any more of our people?" Caine asked any soldier that would listen, but the answer was always negative.

Making their way straight to the rendezvous point they were shocked to see that there was no vessel there. "You do not think it has been destroyed, do you?" Captain Thompson asked Caine.

But at this, exploding out of the water raised a mighty vessel: the HMS Astute, commanded by Captain William George Sheard. The vessel had been hidden on the bottom for over six days now, with protection surrounding it beneath the surface. Captain Sheard had given orders to initiate and follow emergency re-surfacing procedures and to have their precious cargo stored away to re-deploy in record time, as it would not take long to catch the attention of the circling hoards. And he was right. Immediately, all the creatures at Pan's disposal congregated on their position, making it impossible for them to move. Bolt after bolt came flying towards the submarine, as creatures sympathetic to their plight flew in front of them, giving their own lives to ensure the escape of mankind's last hope.

Captain Sheard was waiting to greet our heroes at the main hatch. "I thought I may as well come out for some fresh air, gentlemen," and turning to Captain Thompson, added, "And lady of course. I am afraid that it looks like our time is up. Escape seems somewhat impossible." Looking the rag tag band up and down, Captain Sheard stated, "I am sorry, where are my manners? Have you eaten?" before pointing to the main hatch and beckoning for them to enter.

On the way to the hatch, Danby cut off Captain Sheard and presenting a very poorly Mack, asked, "Please sir. He needs help! Do you have a doctor?"

Captain Sheard looked to his first mate. "Of course. Thomas, would you escort our young friend to Doctor Readman in the infirmary?" Danby flew through the hatch, with the others following the Captain.

Moments after the hatch was shut, one of the sailors shouted to Captain Sheard, "Sir, something's happening sir."

Mother Nature had arrived and had summoned up what seemed to be every flying animal that lived on this green planet: bats, heron, eagles, wrens, sparrows, crows… etc., the list is endless and they were all here at this one point in time. The flying army flew straight into the midst of the battle, blocking out the sun and making the skies thick like porridge.

"This is our chance. Ensign, get us underway immediately."

At that, a giant wave came and lifted them out of the water. Perched on the crest of it, high above the dock as the waters around them gathered and before returning back to the ocean at an incredible speed, with the mighty vessel sat firmly in the wake of the giant mass of water. Poseidon himself was controlling the wave and with a mighty clap of his mighty hands, the god of the deep sent the tidal wave to swallow up the vessel and take it out to safety before their enemies could collect themselves.

Danby had made his way straight to the infirmary with Mack and refused to leave the room whilst Doctor Readman tried in vain to heal the brave little Schmee. "I am sorry son, I am embarrassed to admit it, but I do not know what I am doing. There is nothing I can do for him…I really am sorry! I must now go and see to your friend's arm," he told Danby as he walked out the room to give him time with Mack.

Danby sat over his best friend and whilst trying to fight back his tears once more, he quietly told him, "It will be OK, Mack. I promise. It is simple, I take you to Mother Nature and she will make you all better. You just have to be strong and hold on. Just a little bit longer! Please……? Just hold on!" And holding his tiny little hand, Danby just sat there until he fell to sleep.

Ondre had been taken straight to the infirmary with his badly broken arm, while Danby Senior and the other three had been shown their quarters and took this time to get cleaned up. Meeting with the Captain in the galley afterwards, Captain Thompson, Slick, Caine and Danby Senior took this time to get caught up to date with what was happening in the war with the gods.

"We are losing the battle, I regret to inform you. That was the last of the world's defences gathered in Cape Town and with, from what I witnessed, seventy-five per cent gone." Looking at Danby Senior, Captain Sheard stated, "I just hope that your son is as important as one is lead to believe."

Looking deep into the Captain's eyes, Danby Senior simply replied, "He is to me!"

"So, where is everyone?" Caine asked, breaking the mood.

"There are thousands of little islands scattered throughout the globe and the world is nearly completely covered. The islands that are left are already full past capacity." Bowing his head, Captain Sheard regretfully informed them, "We do not hold out much hope for those poor souls still trapped on the mainland. May God be with them."

At this, Slick piped up, "There's one fing buggin me sir. Wiv no radio, how the hell did yer know we was there?"

Captain Sheard, with a confused look on his face, answered, "I am sorry. After all we have been through over the past weeks, one still does not think that one could ever repeat such nonsense," before raising out of his seat and returning to the bridge.

You see, Captain Sheard had been coordinating his plans with Poseidon and relaying messages through the most beautiful of mermaids. To Captain Sheard, this was just too ridiculous to comprehend. And a story that, I am sure, Captain Sheard would never repeat!

Once the wave had dissipated and left the vessel travelling under its own steam, Captain Sheard looked to his navigator and asked, "Just where the hell are we?"

"About one hundred miles north of our previous location sir," his navigator replied.

"Right, take us to one hundred feet and set course for home, ensign!" The ensign did as he was ordered and the Captain made his way to his quarters, to study his charts and to try and work out just what to do, as the last orders he received were to get his cargo safely back to Saltburn by the sea.

Danby had been asleep by Mack's bedside this whole time and the gang kept checking in on him, but thought it best that he should wake up on his own. When he awoke, his father was sat, keeping a watchful eye on his number one son. Looking immediately at Mack to see if there were any signs of improvement, Danby was broken-hearted to see that there was not. Placing his hands gently on his son's shoulders, Danby Senior spent the next ten minutes trying to persuade his son to go get cleaned up and have some food. "Look son. I will stay here with Mack and I promise you that I will call you if there is any change. No matter how small...... I promise!" Danby was starving and eventually agreed that what his father was saying was right.

In the meantime, Pan was furious at receiving the news of our young hero's escape. There were several gods present and not too happy at being spoken to like children. "Well, what do you expect?" screamed Pan. "With the land, sea and air covered, "could one of you omnipotent beings please explain to me?" And with his hands held out in front of him as if begging and looking around the gods he continued, "Please explain to me how a small mortal child managed to elude and escape you mighty, wise beings? Because I fail to see how it could have happened!"

Loki stepped forward and shrugging his shoulders replied, "Shit happens. Let us move on, shall we? What is important now is to find the child and have him destroyed. Agreed? We have the full Eastern coast completely covered and the rest, patrolling what is left of the coast. I mean, what is with the anger? Job's done! We have caused that much devastation and wiped out a load of them already. Lessons learned and point proven. What if he does get to the bamboo? Saves us a job."

Looking back at Loki and shaking his head in disapproval, Pan informed him, "These parasites have gathered enough knowledge to recreate their ability for worldwide destruction in just a few years. The greed which engulfs them has them so blinded... that they will forget and return back to their old ways, in a matter of no time at all!" Turning his back to them all and bowing his head low, he continued, "I do not like this course and take no pleasure at all in any of this. They are my children too." And turning back around to face the gods, he added, "But we must take away their knowledge and keep a close eye on those that remain. It will take this time of re-evolution for our beautiful home to recover. I regret that we have no other choice."

The other gods looked at each other in agreement, before slowly making their way back to Durnap's realm, which they had been using as a centre of operations.

Back on the HMS Astute, Danby had washed and eaten and on returning to Mack's bedside, he was pleased to see everyone there: Danby Senior, Caine, Slick, Ondre and Captain Thompson. "We have decided you need a nickname like me, Blade an' Slick. Oh and Gorgeous over there," Caine added, pointing in the direction of Captain Thompson, whilst throwing her a cheeky wink. "Well in the letters I have been receiving from home, yer great gran refers to yer as Young Disco as she said she ain't got a clue and daren't imagine what's goin' on under that there 'elmet. So we all agreed that Disco suits and, well, Disco it is." Turning to the rest of them, Caine shouted, "Three cheers for disco!" And all present did just that. Holding on to Mack gently, Disco managed to raise a smile for the first time in far too long.

The gang stayed with Disco and tried their best to raise the mood of our young hero. Disco had no time for frivolity as his best friend was laid there fighting for his life and Disco had to get him home as soon as possible.

Forty minutes or so had elapsed when Captain Sheard entered the room and asked the adults to follow him. Leading them back to the mess and ordering six cups of tea he then asked them to sit. "We have to make a decision, people. We will reach home waters in three days and, taking an educated guess, I assume the whole east coast is a no-go area." Producing a map, Captain Sheard continued, "I think your best bet is for us to drop you off somewhere adjacent on the west coast. We still have no way of contacting anyone and having to do a lot of the navigating old school. My boys are good at what they do, though, and think the best place for a landing is the coastal town of Workington and following the A66 back to home. It will be a long and perilous journey, but safer than staying with us, I feel." The group agreed with Captain Sheard and spent the next couple of hours making plans for their journey home.

Meanwhile back in the examination room, Mack was starting to show signs of life, if not quite coming round. "I will get you home and make you better. I promise!" Danby said softly to his friend tearfully, before Mack slipped back into unconsciousness. Danby cried himself back to sleep whilst cuddling his friend and clinging on to a small hope that Mother Nature and the others could make Mack well again as he was the strongest and bravest being that Danby had ever met. The rest of them were using the remaining time productively in preparation for the journey ahead. Danby never left Mack's side.

CHAPTER XVIII

HE WILL BE OK, WON'T HE?

They had been submerged and travelling homewards for days now, when Captain Sheard had them all meet in the infirmary, as it was easier than peeling Danby away from his sick friend.

"Ladies and gentlemen, we are submerged just off the North East coast of England," Captain Sheard informed them in a very business-like manner and drawing their attention to a map that he was projecting on to the wall. He continued, "We will drop you off here at the town quay and from there it is a short run up Stanley Street to the cover of the railway station. From there you can follow Station Road straight on to the A66, which as you know will lead you straight home." Looking concerned, Captain Sheard leaned on the table in front of them and told them in a stern but worried tone, "I have had a meeting with the crew and it was unanimous that we continue to help as best we can. Once we have seen you safely ashore, we will take the boat and submerge as deep as possible, keeping out of sight of the enemy. Once reaching a believable course set from South Africa to the North East coast of England, the Astute will rise until just visible and hopefully fooling the enemy into believing you are all still travelling on board and hopefully drawing their attentions away from your party. God willing, this will give you a fighting chance. God speed, my friends, and I wish you all luck as I feel you will need it." Captain Sheard saluted the friends and left to arrange their transport to the shore.

Once ashore the group did not wait to see the submarine disembark, and making their way up Station Road immediately headed for the deserted railway station. The blood-curdling shrieks of the Death Breathers echoing through the cold, damp air was the only sound penetrating an eerie and uncomforting silence. Once reaching the station, Danby stood there despondent and tired and yelled, "Stop. Please? Mack does not look well."

"We canna Disco son. We must keep moving. There is nowt we can do for 'im 'ere. Come on son, we gotta get him and us home," Caine told him whilst giving him a quick hug and taking a worried look at the very sick Mack. "Come on son," he repeated whilst heading off in the direction of the others.

Danby's father placed his hand on his shoulder and the pair continued on their way. Reaching the entrance to Station Road, Slick ran outside to the cars deserted out front and checked to see if any of them were open. The shrieks of the Death Breathers were echoing through the air and seeming to get forever closer. Slick managed to get into an old Ford Transit and beckoned the rest to get in. On entering the old Transit, Captain Thompson asked Slick, "Do you think you can get it started?"

Slick just looked back at her and replied, "I'm from the Boro, princess. What do you think?" and at the very second he had finished speaking the old Transit burst into life.

They set off up Station Road at tick-over pace so as not to create too much attention and to limit the noise they made to a minimum. Once hitting the A66, Slick put his foot down and headed straight for his beloved Teesside. They had a run of about an hour before the ghastly shrieks seemed to be on top of them. Suddenly an explosion rocked the van. "I think they might have found us," Ondre stated.

"It's OK. They can't know it's us and if we can lose them they might just give up. Wythop Woods are just a few miles up the road, so just try and keep us on the road till then Slick me old mucka." Patting Slick on the shoulder, Caine was thrown against the van and landed in Captain Thompson's lap as the explosions got more frequent. Caine just smiled at the Captain and whilst raising his eyebrows, simply said "Hello" in a seductive manner. Captain Thompson just smiled and threw him off. The explosions however were quickly becoming too much for Slick to handle.

"Look, the woods. Get us in there Slick and we might have a fighting chance in amongst the trees," screamed Caine with explosions raining down all around them.

Slick bobbed and weaved with his foot flat to the floor. Reaching the Lake District and getting in among the trees the gang abandoned the van and continued their journey on foot. Keeping in the thick of the trees and hearing deafening explosions all around them, the gang were stuck for ideas and just tried to get as far away from the explosions as possible. Keeping Disco safe was everyone's main priority and they all knew that it was wiser to get back on course once it was safe. Twenty minutes or so elapsed, which seemed like an eternity to our weary heroes, before the enemy above started to disperse. Looking around for any signs of the enemy, Slick told the others, "I reckon we should sit tight for a bit and go an' find the 66 again." The gang made themselves comfortable and took this time to collect their thoughts.

After a couple of long hours, Caine piped up, "I think we better get a move on. It's getting dark." Caine had taken this time to study the map and piece together some kind of half-hearted plan. "Right, if we head back on ourselves we should come across the Pheasant Inn. We can spend the night there and see if there's owt to eat as I don't know 'bout you lot but I'm sick of these ere MREs."

The gang all agreed and started back in the direction they had just come from. Reaching the Pheasant Inn they were surprised to find people still living there: Steve and Dianne Nicholson. On approaching the Inn there were no lights and the place looked to be abandoned but on further inspection Danby Senior caught a glimpse of a gas fire glowing gently in one of the back rooms. Making their way around the back of the Inn, Captain Thompson knocked gently on the door. A stocky man answered, about medium height and with a shaved head and shotgun. "Can I help you?" he asked whilst looking down the barrel of the gun.

"We are sorry to disturb you," Captain Thompson said. "We are just looking for somewhere warm to spend the night."

Steve looked them up and down and lowering his gun beckoned them in. Walking them through to the kitchen, Steve gestured towards the cooker and informed them, "This is the missus, Di."

Di was a petite woman with long brown hair and a constant smile. "Well sit yourselves down then," she ordered whilst filling the kettle from the sink. "Cuppa? You all look like you could do with one. Who are you? What you doin' out here? You hungry? Where y' from?" Di spluttered out before Steve stopped her: "Take a breath woman. Leave them alone." And whilst shaking his head with a smile on his face he added, "You'll have to excuse Di. She wants to know the ins and outs of a fart."

Di screamed "Steve!" and laughed as she went to the fridge from which she produced bacon, sausage and black pudding. "Six breakfasts it is then. No one is vegetarian are you? No? Good." And off she went cooking a meal for our heroes.

After eating and washing up everyone went into the dining room and sat by the fire. "What you got there?" Di asked Danby.

"It's my friend Mack. He's been injured trying to protect us," and with floods of tears streaming down his face he murmured, "I just want him to wake up... He won't wake up." To which Di started crying herself and made immediately for our young hero to wrap her arms around him and comfort this heartbroken child.

Meanwhile the HMS Astute had reached the decoy course and was slowly commencing to rise to a visible but believable depth. It took less than an hour for the enemy to spot them and as Captain Sheard predicted, all hell broke loose, with creatures of the wildest imagination encroaching on them whilst evil and remorseless dragons fired explosive bolts and dived into the deep cold water trying to reach them and rip the vessel to tiny little bits.

"Dive ensign, dive. Get us out of here," Captain Sheard screamed with explosions pounding the water and tearing the vessel to bits. "Fire everything we have, none nuclear, the radiation would reach the shores.. If we are to go down gentlemen, we are to go down kicking and screaming. For Queen and country, boys, we have a little boy to help get home." And with explosions rattling the ship whilst creatures of the deep pounding at the hull, Captain Sheard just smiled at his bridge crew, raised an eyebrow and calmly said, "Give them hell and do your country proud!"

The battle raged on for several hours, lighting up the sea and sky alike. Like the most expensive fireworks display ever mounted and no one there to witness it. I do not know just what end awaited the brave Captain Sheard and his crew but Danby and his companions would never forget what the HMS Astute had done for them.

It was cracking on for four-thirty and Caine had started to wake everyone. "Come on, it's time we made a move."

Once awake the gang sat and tried to develop a plan. At that Diane came through. "I thought I had heard you all stirring. Cuppa before you go? Go on. It will only take a minute." And she made her way towards the sink with kettle in hand.

"Thank you. Please," Captain Thompson said with a gentle smile. "Thank you for everything. You have been really kind."

Don't be daft," Diane replied. "It has been a pleasure. You just make sure you that you all take care of that young fella and his, well you know? His thingymajig." And looking confused, she just added, whilst flicking her left arm in the air, "You know what I mean. Just look after them two." And she carried on to make the tea, gently shaking her head and chortling to herself.

Steve was up about twenty minutes later as the gang were just finishing up and preparing to leave. "Glad I caught yer. Look, me and the missus were talking last night and we have the two cars out there. Well it doesn't look like they will be much use to us at the mo, so you may as well take the Defender. Look after her, as she's never let me down. Good luck to us all and let us hope this nightmare's soon over." Ruffling Disco's hair, Steve added, "Look after yourself, ickle fella, and for God's sake stay safe." Passing Caine the keys, Steve went on to pour a cup of tea.

"Look, we really do owe you both an enormous debt of gratitude. Thank you both so very much. Nice to see there are still decent people in these desperate times. Thank you!" Caine said before grabbing his rifle and making his way to the door with the rest following.

Getting outside the gang made their way to the garage where they found a small Nissan and the Land Rover Defender. Passing the keys to Slick, Caine and the rest got in.

"How we doing for fuel Slick?" Caine asked.

"Nearly a full tank, scored," replied Slick.

Looking round with a cheeky smile on his face, Caine looked to Ondre and asked, "You OK there, son? You look a bit pale."

Ondre just gave Caine a "whatever"-type smile and the gang got the car from the garage, closed up and got on their way. Making their way across country and keeping out of sight of aerial predators, progress was slow but at least they were heading in the right direction and getting ever closer.

Back at Durnap's lair the gods were gathering and keenly anticipating the arrival of Pan in order to gloat and tell him that Danby was no longer a problem. Anubis was getting restless. "Where he is and who does he think he is to keep gods waiting like nothing but common knaves?!" At that, Pan burst in to the room with Durnap by his side. Durnap made his way towards Anubis and looked him up and down with an utter look of contempt.

"Why you impudent little garden gnome. Who do you think you are to look at your master in such a fashion?" Anubis screamed whilst raising his arm to smite Durnap.

Eros reached over and grabbing Anubis's arm simply looked straight at Anubis and shook his head gently. "Have we finished yet, children, or shall we leave it until playtime?"

Pan said in a stern voice, "So where are we on the human child that holds the gods to ransom? Good news one hopes gentlemen?"

Hephaestus stepped forwards and with a smug look perched firmly on his face told Pan, "The child has been destroyed. The explosion which ensued made it nigh on impossible to find any remains... But we are continuing the search."

And the shard?" asked Pan.

"Not a chance," piped up Loki. "Looking for a tiny, little piece of wood, on a wreckage-strewn across the ocean floor with currents that could pull an island from its own foundations! Yeah, right. Good luck with that."

"Loki's right," added Hermes. "You will just have to do with the havoc our forces and the bamboo combined have brought upon mankind. Either way we come out winners."

And looking around with a not very confident look upon his face, Loki asked the others, "Do we not?"

"Until I see the young mortal strewn out before me or some definite proof that he was still even on the vessel the search continues. Do you all understand? I want that child. Dead or alive, I want that child." At that Pan turned to the grand doors of the hall and made his way toward them. "If you have news that will please me, please do not hesitate to get in touch. Otherwise please leave me to my thoughts. I have a lot to plan for the future of mankind," he said in an arrogant tone as he stepped through the enormous doors. The gods stuck around for nearly an hour before agreeing on what to do next in the hunt for our hero Disco Danby.

Back in the mortal realm Disco and the others were finding it progressively harder to evade their pursuers, as for some reason they had seemed to have taken the search up a notch. Keeping just off of the A66 the gang were just coming to a place called Saddleback View when they saw a dark cloud of the enemy's number one search and destroy weapon, Death Breathers and dozens of them, whilst the fields on the other side of the A66 where awash with a wide array of creatures, and all heading their way. Making their way towards three houses just a few hundred metres in front of them, Slick pulled in to Troutbeck Camp and Caravan Club which was full of abandoned lime-green holiday homes. The gang abandoned the Land Rover and made their way into one of the holiday homes, keeping as silent as possible, and all were getting more and more worried about their brave little friend Mack as his breathing had been getting worse for some time now. They had been hiding for over an hour whilst the shrieks got ever louder and the sound of movement outside had started to become somewhat familiar when loud roars were to be heard and what sounded like a massive battle raged outside. Terrified, the gang just laid low and waited for whatever was going on outside to run its course, but that plan was foiled when what was left of an enormous wolf came crashing through the window of the chalet.

"What the hell is going on out there?" Caine shouted as he made his way stealthily towards the hole that used to be the window. Looking out Caine was shocked to see a vicious battle going on outside. Giant creatures that could only be described as giant mole-looking, with muscles which looked like they were about to rip through the thick leathery skin and long teeth about eight inches long and razor-sharp-looking whilst entangled and downright terrifying, were pulling the Death Breathers out of the air with ferocious ease and a military-type execution.

Suddenly one of these creatures ripped the door with its frame clean from the side of the holiday home. Slick and Ondre trained their weapons straight toward the beast when Disco screamed, "No...... Stop." And throwing himself between himself and the creature, he continued, "It's Maschmee. It's Mack's mother." And turning to face her and with floods of tears Disco held out her son and apologized repeatedly for what had happened to him.

Maschmee bent down to see her son and gently stroked his cheek with her massive talon before screaming a deafening cry into the sky and then looking motionless at her sick son Mack. Standing there staring at her son for what must have been seconds but felt like an eternity, Disco swore he could see the anger building through her body before she looked him in the eye and took off, wreaking a revenge on their enemies that only a grieving mother would understand.

Once the battle had slowed down and there were only a few creatures left, a dozen or so of Mack's kind gathered in the campsite while Maschmee returned to claim her ailing son. Meeting her out the front and keeping Mack as warm and comfortable as he possibly could, Disco handed his friend back to his own kind. As soon as Maschmee had Mack in her arms she instantly jumped into the air followed by the rest of her kind and was at least a mile away in a matter of seconds.

"Wait…Stop…What about us?" Caine shouted behind them but to no avail as the Schmee were deaf to their calls and had their minds set on one thing only: getting Mack home and making him well again.

"Charmin…What a bloody cheek," Caine muttered as he walked back to the Land Rover with his hands in his pockets and kicking stones like a child that had not just gotten his own way.

"Looks like we're on us tod," piped up Ondre.

CHAPTER XIX

LET US JUST CONCENTRATE ON
GETTING YER HOME!

Disco collapsed on the steps of the chalet, broken-hearted. "Come on son, this is your time to show how strong you really are," Danby Senior told his boy whilst wrapping his arms around him and squeezing him tight. Struggling to control his emotions himself at the sight of his son hurting so much, Danby Senior took a deep breath and continued, "Come on son... Mack was hurt trying to help us... If you give up now Mack will have been hurt for nothing and I do not think that anyone wants or expects that from you, so pick yourself up son and let's finish what you and Mack started together."

Disco just sat there in his father's arms for a good five minutes, thinking about what his father had just told him, before getting up, wiping his eyes and asking everyone, "Well...? What are you all waiting for?" and climbing into the Land Rover with his sulking uncle Caine.

"You did the right thing, you know," Captain Thompson told Danby Senior on their way to the vehicle.

"So why is it that I feel I have just placed my son in harm's way?" Danby Senior replied before walking off and climbing into the adjacent door. It was a tight squeeze in the Land Rover Defender but at least the heater worked and it was much more suitable than walking.

No one spoke as they set off as they were all too busy watching the horizon for more Death Breathers and other creatures brought to the surface by the angry gods. They were right to be vigilant as an army of amphibious creatures were making their way from Ullswater towards Penrith and the A66 that they were travelling home on. These creatures were an ancient race that normally scoured the ocean floors looking for plunder and the greatest of deaths: the Grendlar, powerful and remorseless, warlike creatures that became involved just to immerse themselves in the glory of the battle. Powerful creatures, half-man, half-serpent, with armoured scales and rows of razor-sharp teeth that took up most of its round, football-shaped head. Unawares, our heroes were heading straight for them.

As they approached Penrith there was an eerie silence. All was still and even the wind seemed absent. Slick was trying to avoid the city and make his way around when from nowhere a Grendlar landed on the bonnet and smashed his hand like claws through the windscreen at Slick.

"Bloody hell. Shoot it, shoot it," Slick screamed as he put his foot down and tried to shake it off.

Disco had seen a half-full bottle of perfume which must have belonged to Mrs Nicholson in the car door and reached straight for it. Diving over Slick's shoulder, Disco squirted the perfume into the creature's face and was amazed to see it work like acid on the sea-dwelling creature. Caine took this opportunity to lift his legs through what was left of the windscreen and kick out at the creature until it was eventually thrown from the bonnet. More and more of these evil-looking creatures were just appearing from nowhere and forcing the gang into Penrith.

"Quick, head for the hospital," screamed Caine as the creatures had started to throw what looked like giant shells covered in thick, gooey mucus which adhered to whatever it touched and continued on to explode. Trying his hardest to avoid the creatures, Slick made his way towards the hospital. The noise in the Land Rover was unbearable with guns and screaming. Disco had to cover his ears and just kept his head down as instructed whilst waiting for the order to abandon the vehicle. On reaching the front of the hospital Caine kicked his door open and kept screaming, "Out, out, out," whilst making his way towards the big glass doors which were the way in to the building. "Locked," said Caine before lowering his rifle and pointing his sidearm at the door he fired two shots into it, causing it to cascade down just like the glass had been turned to liquid. "Quickly," Caine shouted whilst beckoning everyone in with his left arm which still held his pistol.

Suddenly a creature appeared and grabbed Disco, at which Caine raised his arm and fired a shot clean between the creature's eyes. The creature just stood there motionless for a short while before falling to the floor. With a smile beaming from ear to ear and a smug look on his face, Caine strutted through the door saying, "Now that's Teesside aggro."

With explosions all around them the team took cover in the main foyer and made whatever barricades they could. Swarms of Grendlar came flooding through the doors as Caine and the others tried in vain to hold them back. "Fall back. Fall back," Caine said, and continued to hold his position until the others had started their retreat down the corridor. "Quick the staircase," Caine instructed everyone and pushed everyone in as he thought it would be best if he could funnel the enemy. "Danby, Get our Disco to the roof and wait there for us," Caine told Danby Senior whilst passing him his sidearm. Danby Senior gave Caine an agreeing nod and continued to lead Disco towards the roof and hopefully away from the danger for the time being.

On reaching the roof they were met by a heavily padlocked door. Danby Senior paced up and down trying to think whilst the hospital shook with the sounds of gunfire and explosions. Danby Senior stopped dead, stared at the pistol in his hand and shrugging his shoulders, lifted his hand and shot the mighty padlock. Disco looked at his father and informed him that he had missed. Danby Senior took the weapon in both hands at this and with his tongue sticking out with concentration he fired several shots at the padlock until he was sure he had hit it. The padlock was still intact and Danby Senior was starting to get frustrated. "Quick, the top floor, there must be a fire escape. Come on; let us have a look son." As he made his way down the stairs Disco started to follow.

Meanwhile back in the realm of Mother Nature, gods and creatures alike were willing Mack to recover as no Schmee had died in thousands of years and they were all determined to make sure Mack was not to be the first. To no avail, though, as the Death Breathers had done too much damage and Mack was slowly slipping away. Thousands of Schmee had congregated at Mack's bedside: all his brothers and sisters, in fact there was not a Schmee living that was not there wishing their brother to be well.

At this time back in the mortal realm Disco's father had found the fire escape and ushered Disco up in front of him. On the way to the roof Danby Senior spotted an old YZ 250 laid on its side in the car park, just like the carving which was broken by Disco's brothers and laid so freshly in Danby Senior's memory, as to him it was not so long ago. "Danby, I have an idea. Come on," and Danby Senior started to make his way down the steps. Disco followed.

Suddenly Disco collapsed and at that very moment a soul-destroying howl echoed across the planet as the Schmee had realized that Mack had passed on into the land of Papaschmee: the father of all Schmee, lover of Maschmee and the first Schmee to fall in battle, who was believed to be sat waiting on his wife and children in a glorious land of no evil. Danby Senior had tears in his eyes and did not know why as he picked up his son and placed him in safety behind some large galvanized bins at the bottom of the steps before stepping out into the car park to see if he could get the bike started. Weaving his way through parked and deserted traffic, Danby Senior reached the bike. A makeshift ignition had been fitted to the bike but Danby Senior knew how to get round this. Working on the bike as quickly as he could, Danby Senior pushed the bike as quietly as possible to his son, hoping to have his son sat securely on the bike before attracting the attention of the sea creatures which were working as mercenaries for Pan and the other gods.

Disco was coming back round on his return. "You OK, son? What happened?" Danby senior asked as he helped his boy back to his feet.

"It's Mack I think. He's dead. I could feel it," Disco said, looking to be in shock. "Let's get home and try to put an end to this shall we?" he said with an angry and vengeful look on his face which made his father worried.

Danby Senior kicked the bike over again and again but with no joy. The noise from this attracted the attention of the Grendlar and Danby Senior knew this as he kicked harder and harder. Suddenly the bike exploded to life and Disco jumped on just in time as one of the creatures had reached him and he had escaped capture by mere millimetres. Heading parallel with the A66 Danby Senior set off cross-country with his son and leaving the others behind. Weaving between monsters and explosions Danby Senior did what he did best and got his son out of there. With shrieks of Death Breathers getting closer Danby Senior focused his attentions on losing his pursuers and getting under cover. They managed this and ended up taking shelter in Crowdundle Woods and hiding there until nightfall.

Back at the hospital, Caine and the others were searching for Disco and his father and were under the presumption that they had been captured. After a brief discussion it was decided that they should set off in pursuit of the Grendlar to rescue Disco and his father.

Once nightfall arrived Danby Senior waited for the Death Breathers' shrieks to be as far away as possible. "You ready son?" he asked Disco before starting the bike and making his way to Appleby to try and find fuel. Danby Senior knew Appleby as he and Disco's mother had visited a big gypsy fair which is held annually on a couple of occasions when they were courting and before Disco was even thought of.

On reaching the Gulf garage down by the bridge in Appleby, Danby Senior was frustrated to find the pumps and garage locked up securely. Pulling out the pistol and aiming it at the lock on the pump Danby Senior went to blast the lock off. Looking at Disco, Danby Senior told him, "Not the best idea, methinks." And looking across the road he smiled and started to walk towards the Westmorland Building Centre and using the pistol as a club Danby Senior smashed the glass front and after disappearing inside for several minutes he reappeared waving a crowbar in his right hand. After getting the fuel and oil that they needed, Disco and his father set off back on their journey.

Caine and the others in the meantime had tracked the Grendlar back to Ullswater and were trying to work out how to follow underwater.

"We could turn a row boat upside down and walk the lake floor. I've seen it in loads of films. Yeah? What yer think?" Ondre piped up.

"The boat will float, muppet," Slick said laughingly and shaking his head.

"Na, that's it. We can't follow 'em any further. We'll just 'ave to go to me gran's in Saltburn and hope they're on their way there too," Caine added before picking up his kit and walking off to the east in the direction of his family home.

Disco and his dad were making their way along the A66 once again when from nowhere they came across a patrol of Death Breathers and with explosions rampaging all around the pair were forced to take cover in Barnard Castle, riding through the streets like a man possessed, trying to avoid their pursuers and cutting through parks looking for cover in which to hide. With the beasts above proving impossible to lose, Danby Senior decked the bike and dragged Disco through back gardens and hedges until he felt confident that they had lost their deadly followers. Seeing a sign for Darlington which was a place Danby Senior had a little knowledge of, his spirits felt slightly lifted. "Come on son. I think we would be wise to travel on foot for a while. At least until those ruddy things have decided that they have lost us," he told Disco whilst grabbing his shoulder and pulling him along the side of the A67 to Darlington.

As Disco and his dad started on the final leg of their journey back to Saltburn, things had hit an all-time low in the immortal realms. It may have only been a couple of hours for Disco and the others, but in Mother Nature's realm nearly two weeks had passed and it was time for the funeral of their fallen hero. The procession made its way through Mother Nature's courtyard with Mack swaddled tightly in a linen cloth and levitating about six inches from the floor so that his family could approach the body and give their respects. On leaving through the mighty gates of Mother Nature's palace to make their way onto her mighty galleon to transport Mack to his final resting place with the other fallen Schmee, everybody was shocked to see Pan and the other opposing gods. In a split-second Maschmee and the others had transformed into their defensive shape, just like the one witnessed by our heroes earlier at Saddleback View. Diving at the gods and pinning them to the floor, Mother Nature shouted, "STOP... Let them up. Please my friends, let them rise?"

Maschmee took ten or so seconds before releasing the god she blamed for the death of her son and she made her way to Mack. Lifting him into her arms, Maschmee just sat and cuddled her son, totally oblivious to everything else around her.

"Why are you here Pan? What do you want here?"

Pan bowed his head in shame before lifting his head and looking firmly into Mother Nature's eyes and telling her firmly, "We have come to pay our respects. The Schmee, like it or not, are our friends too. For thousands of years we have lived side by side and shared our lives with each other. We did not want this and feel sad for the loss but war brings heartbreak. You brought this on by splitting from us and taking the side of those... Those... Parasites. We will take our leave now, but remember, my sister." And starting to turn to leave, Pan added, "You split the family."

As Pan left Mother Nature told him, "I cannot sit and watch you spread your evil. You are wrong Pan and mankind deserves a chance to change their ways, not the evil you have forced upon them. You are wrong and you have taken many lives. I am ashamed to call you of my kind." Bowing her head Mother Nature turned towards Maschmee and her dead son and walking towards her heartbroken friend, Mother Nature told Pan and his group over her shoulder, "I think you should go."

Mother Nature placed her hand on Maschmee's shoulder and told her, "I am sorry my friend but we must talk once your son is reunited with his father." Maschmee simply looked at Mother Nature and slowly blinked in agreement.

On returning from the funeral, Mother Nature walked Maschmee into the great hall and sat down. Maschmee, who was now back into her natural form, sat with a very heavy heart and listened intently to what her friend had to say. "I am sorry my friend but I must ask you to place one more of your children in harm's way. Danby, when he returns, will still need our help. I would not ask this if it was not important to what is going on."

Maschmee just looked at Mother Nature with a confused look on her face and stormed out of the great hall as fast as her little legs would carry her. Mother Nature just sat there regretting the fact that she had upset her old friend and trying to work out what to do from here. Ten or so minutes had passed when the door to the great hall opened ever so slightly and in walked Maschmee and another of her children.

"Tackschmee, my old friend, I am so sorry for the loss of your brother but thank you for taking his place. He died for a good cause and made us all so very, very proud," said Mother Nature, and looking in the direction of Maschmee, she added, "Maschmee… Thank you, I know it must be hard but we need the schmee's help now more than ever. Danby, if he returns, must never find out the fate of Mack. He is still a child with such a heavy weight upon his shoulders… This may be one too many battles for his young head to comprehend. I am sorry to disrespect Mack's memory but I find this the best course of action." Maschmee and Tack just nodded their heads and took their leave.

Caine and the others by this time were not a million miles from Disco and his father as they made their way across the A66, which may as well have been a million miles as both groups had no way of contacting the other and giving their position. Daybreak was only a couple of hours away and the blood-curdling shrieks of the Death Breathers echoed closer and more frequently.

"We must find somewhere to rest," said Caine as he got his map and compass out of his hip pocket. Studying the map, he added, "I think our best bet is to get off the road and follow the Tees. It will take us straight to Redcar and give us better cover. Just a few miles from here is Wycliffe Hall. There has got to be some scran there." Looking at the others he was greeted with no opposition, so picking himself up Caine started making his way towards the hall.

Danby Senior had had a similar idea and was now looking out for somewhere the pair could rest and hopefully get food and drink. After an hour or so of looking and not long before sunrise Danby Senior found the perfect place: hidden in trees and just off the road lay Stubb House Lodge. Danby and Disco checked the place out for ten minutes or so before deciding that the place was empty. The pair made their way straight to the rear of the house, looking for the kitchen and somewhere to break in without causing too much damage or noise. Both teams had reached and gained entry into their resting places for the next few hours and after eating their fill they all got their heads down and got some much needed rest.

Caine and Danby Senior had both decided to follow the Tees River and wait for dusk before they would make their move for home. After looking for things of use, Danby Senior found a samurai sword, an aluminium baseball bat which he gave to Disco and a small pit bag which he filled with as many snacks as he could come upon and whatever bottles he could find to put water in. "Away then lad. We better get a shift on," Danby Senior told Disco before stepping outside and checking to see the coast was clear. Disco followed his father outside and the pair made their way towards the river on their way back to Saltburn. Caine and the others were searching the hall for useful items before leaving to follow the river home and once they were sure there was nothing else worth taking they set off on their way.

Danby Senior and Caine were travelling on opposite sides of the river for five or six hours now before coming across Gainford which is a quite picturesque little village by the banks of the Tees. Caine and the others crossed a small bridge and entered Gainford cautiously and made their way down the A67 which passed through the centre of the village. About one hundred and fifty meters in on the right, Captain Thompson saw a Cross Keys on the right and suggested that this may be a good place to rest.

Ondre piped up, "Good idea Cap, coz I is starvin'."

"You're always starving," added Slick as Dre set off in the direction of the public house, scratching inside his pot with a small branch he had snapped off a tree earlier.

Once there, Ondre looked through the window and instantly fell to one knee whilst gesturing that his friends should follow suit. Crawling through the car park, his friends caught Dre up. "What's wrong fella?" Caine asked.

"People, mate. Twenty or so people sat by the fire."

Standing up Caine told Dre laughingly, "Christ, man. We're not at war with these people." And whilst the others got to their feet, Caine banged on the window. A large biker-looking man with short greying hair and a goatee came to unlock the door.

"Well, if it ain't four of our country's finest. My name's Baz Donegue." And stepping back he gestured that the four of them come in before adding, "Get yourselves by the fire... Please make yourselves at home."

On entering the bar area, Caine was shocked to hear "Uncle Caine...Uncle Caine." And running out from a seat by the fire, a white motocross helmet came flying towards him. "Uncle Caine, it's you," screamed Disco as he flung his arms around him. Danby Senior had made his way over if not quite so emphatically and held his hand out as he approached.

"What happened?" asked Caine.

"Come, sit by the fire and I'll tell you," Danby senior replied.

The six of them introduced themselves to the locals and made their way to a table large enough for them all. Danby Senior and Disco had been explaining what had gone on for only five or so minutes when Baz came over with drinks and a few bags of crisps, scratchings and salted peanuts. "Here you are. On the house," the monster of a man told them.

"Baz is from Redcar," Disco told the others.

"Well, Marske, about a mile down the road from there but I live in Redcar now with the missus, Zel. Bet she's getting worried by now, like," he replied.

"So what yer doin' ere?" Slick asked.

"Well I was out for a ride when all this kicked off and one of them bloody flying demons forced me off the road. Old Kev Wright over there somehow managed to drag me here. Bad back an' all. Could have saved me life, I reckon." He pointed to a man at the bar, holding his pint aloft with a crooked back and a massive smile on his face.

"Look it's startin' to tank it down. Stay until it stops. I don't think anyone will mind," said Baz before taking a large swig of his pint.

""Who are all these people?" asked Captain Thompson.

"This lot?" Baz replied whilst pointing over his shoulder. "This lot are just locals who refuse to let the beasties spoil their night."

Captain Thompson laughed and stated, "Sometimes you feel really proud to be British! Eh?"

"Christ. Have yer seen the rain out there?" Slick asked the others whilst mesmerized by how heavy the rain was outside.

"I think we might just take you up on that offer to stay a while. Till that rain dies down at least," Caine said, with everybody else nodding emphatically. This was to take longer than anyone thought.

After a day of constant heavy rain and no reprieve becoming apparent, the gang thought it looked very likely that they were going to get wet.

"Bloody British summer. You ain't thinking 'bout taking me out there are you? I'm injured remember" Dre said to Caine holding his broken arm up and gesturing towards it.

"Sorry people. We've been here far too long already."

As these words came from his mouth there was the sound of thunder in the distance. But this thunder was not going to cease, as in the last twenty-four hours a lot had happened, both in the immortal realms and here on Earth. Mother Nature had spent the morning coordinating creatures of the Earth and those of fact and fiction before making her way to a supposedly secret location deep in the bowels of the Earth to talk to the British premiers of this time, David Cameron and Nick Clegg. These three had been in conference prior to the world's armies converging on Cape Town to help our heroes home but no one had informed her to where the premiers were at this moment and that made them very concerned. After stepping into the conference room full of Britain's most powerful men as if from nowhere, Mother Nature was surprised to be set upon by the security present.

"Stop!" David Cameron shouted. "Stand down."

Walking towards the shocked Mother Nature and ushering her into a quiet room behind them he went in after her , followed by his cohort Nick Clegg.

Once the door was shut David Cameron told her in a raised firm voice, "What the hell, your Majesty…Highness or Mam? Or whatever the hell I should call you." And lowering his tone he continued, "I am sorry about my men but you cannot just walk in here without announcement. You are more than welcome but… Well… you must understand. Once again, we are so very sorry but what can we do for you?"

Still looking shocked but in a strong, business-like voice she told him, "The others, Pans armies, have picked up the search of the northeast coast, which means Danby must be avoiding them still, and from what Mascmee has informed me he must be getting close. I am coordinating defences from the entrance of my realm to help the child home and it would be in your best interests to help him to safety as he and the shard must not end up in Pan's grasp. This would mean dire consequences for the peoples of the world and reduce the people of your island further into servitude to the gods. We must launch an all-out defensive and get the child safely into my realm where we can take over and do what must be done."

David stood for several seconds and turned to Nick who was just sat there listening to what Mother Nature had to say and ushered him into the furthest corner to talk in private. Turning towards the mother god, David told her, "We agree with you and will do all that we can," whilst Nick opened the door and shouted to the officials outside, "Get me a message to every man, woman and child that can bear arms to converge on Teesside. We need to throw everything we have into that area. Please gentlemen, this is of an urgent nature." And closing the door behind him Nick turned to Mother Nature with a smile on his face and claimed, "I hope you are right about this boy as we have the Olympics in a little over three months and the British do like to keep a promise."

Mother Nature looked at him confused and took her leave as she still had a lot to do in the mystic realms. On returning home Mother Nature was shocked yet pleased to find that the Holly King had been located and woken and brought to her. "Holly King my old friend," Mother Nature said as she held her arms out to welcome her old friend. "I am so glad to see you. I assume you are up to date with what is going on? We need you to help hold back the evil vine that is engulfing the planet. I know you don't get on but your brother the Oak King is already helping by the use of the sun's rays but if you could travel to the other side of the world and use the cold to slow its progress that would help immensely."

"I am sorry my old friend, but I am not decided on whose actions I agree on. Mankind has systematically destroyed this planet for what has been the last twelve hundred years to us gods. And we have had the misfortune to have been able to watch all this in slow motion. I am sorry my friend, but I have come to tell you in person that I am going to keep out of this. My mind is made up, I am sorry but I must leave now as I have sleep to catch up on." And as he left the great hall, he stopped, looked back and repeated, "Once again, I really am sorry my friend."

Mother Nature just stood silent with a disappointed look on her face and simply replied, "I understand."

Once dusk had come, Disco and the others started back on their journey home in the pouring rain. They had agreed that it was much safer to continue on foot but Dre wanted it to be taken into consideration that a vehicle was quicker, dryer, warmer and just down right better than the God-awful British Weather. The fact that the group was soaked already stood testament to the fact he never got his own way. It did not take long for them to work out that it was not thunder they were hearing as the explosions could be seen for miles. A mighty battle was raging over Teesside and right along the eastern coast.

"Bloody hell," muttered Slick. "Would you take a look at that?"

Explosions lit up the night sky all across the region as whatever armies and civilians that could be mustered fought alongside Mother Nature's allies to try and divert Pan's forces' attentions to hopefully give Disco and his friends a clear run for home. Both sides were taking a pounding as the heavens opened, lightning and explosions alike, lighting up the evening skies and throwing out silhouettes of raging battles between good and evil.

"Dre my friend. It looks like you are about to get your wish." And running back to the Cross Keys, Caine burst in and shouted, "We need transport. Does anyone have anything we can use?"

Looking out the back, Baz came storming through holding a set of keys: "Here, take these." And throwing the keys to Caine, Baz explained, "There is a minibus in the garage out back. Should be OK as no one's seen the landlord or his missus in days. Don't even know if they're the keys but an educated guess says they are."

And as Caine turned to leave, an old woman grabbed at his arm and as he turned she said softly, "Safe journeys son and I hope you reach the end of whatever it is you're up too. All of you be safe."

Caine made his way straight to the garage and was pleased to see the keys were the right ones. Driving it out and moving over to give Slick the driving seat, Caine was getting quite excited about getting Disco safe and re-joining whatever was left of his regiment to get stuck back in.

Getting back on the A67 and with no lights, the speeds Slick was driving had the others a bit worried. Slick could sense this though and found it quite a giggle. It did not take long before the gang met the action as units of British, French and Belgian soldiers and artillery were being held by the enemy. Stopping by a Challenger 2, Slick tried to find out what was going on, but with explosions, gunfire and the shrieks of the enemy, Slick could not hear a thing. "Well only one thing for it," Slick told the others. "Look, I know this area like the back of my hand. I reckon we should fly up Stockton Road and floor it up the 66 until we reach our destination. I can do it and can't think of a better plan...... Anyone else think of owt better? No? Let's crack on then."

Slick floored the minibus and set off on the final leg of their journey before the others had time to answer. With the dark, wet night sky lit up by the battle, everyone thought this was a spectacular sight with the silhouettes of machine and demon making war in amongst the clouds but terrifying as the explosions got closer and closer, rocking the van and throwing it across the road. Once on the 66 it soon became very open and uninviting but luckily, even though being pursued, with what was left of all the world's forces army, navy and air force attacking at every opportune moment, Disco and his companions were not a main priority. Things would change if the enemy knew who was travelling in the three-year-old pub minibus.

They had barely made it to Southbank after luckily escaping several attacks, when the road just disappeared. The British Steel and ICI buildings, or what was left of them, were strewn all over and a giant crater lay where they both stood. Slick did a U-turn and headed towards Normanby Road and headed up it on an alternative route, but the entrance to Durnap's realm lay just beyond the end of this road and his Dwarf hordes had made their way into the Southbank and Grangetown area to wreak havoc and have fun at the expense of the locals. Things were not going to plan, though, as these Teessiders had more fight in them than Durnap's men had anticipated. Unfortunately for the invading force, these people quite enjoyed a good kick-off. Golf clubs, baseball bats and anything else man, woman or child could pick up were being used to hold back these intruders and protect what was left of their homes, as for most of them, this was all they had. Seeing these people holding back their attackers in such a way picked up the gang's spirits and made them feel quite proud to belong to this nation of people.

Slick thought that the only way to carry on in the vehicle was to cut through the hills on Flats Lane and join the A171 which runs past Guisborough (ancient capital of the north), which would take them into Saltburn the back way. The enemies were attacking them in scores the closer they got to home. With what was left of the world's forces defending the entrance to Mother Nature's realm and creatures of fact and fantasy spewing out of the entrance set firmly in the cliff front to join the battle, everyone thought the entrance to the realm would be easy. Reaching there would be a totally different matter, though.

Pan was in Durnap's great hall watching the battle for Teesside and laughing a gut-busting laugh at the antics of the mighty dwarf armies getting their behinds handed to them by these mere mortals and in a more and more organized way. "Whooo hooo hoo," Pan was in fits of laughter as gangs of young children chased small groups of Durnap's men round the streets. "I am sorry my loyal friend... But if you could step back." And Pan could speak no more for gut-busting laughter.

Durnap gave Pan a look of discontent and stormed out of the hall as quickly as his little legs could carry him as high-pitched sounds of "No please. Come back, I'm sorry" teemed through the corridor. It was fair to say that Durnap's men were not doing as well as he thought they would. Pan's forces were not doing much better as they were starting to be held back. Thousands of creatures fought in the air, sea and on land. Creatures of myth and legend greeted Disco and the others at every turn now as you could not avoid large groups of soldiers and large artillery. With dragons and other creatures falling from the sky and the constant attack from wild animals coming from the hills, no one could predict at the minute in whose favour things were going to turn.

Meanwhile Danby and the others were making their way through immense battles as they travelled down Hob Hill Lane and no more than a mile away from Mother Nature and what felt like safety, when suddenly a large number of stone-like spears hit the right hand side of the minibus and with enough power to send the minibus rolling off of the road. After a good ten seconds of confusion and disarray Caine finally shouted out, "What the hell happened...? Is everyone OK?" and kicking what was left of the windscreen out, he took his leave of the vehicle and took cover behind it whilst trying to assess the situation and work out just who had attacked them. Banging on the roof of the van as it lay on its side, Caine repeated his question: "Is everyone OK? Come on people, I need you out the van now."

Slick was the next to emerge and took his place by Caine's side and as the rest scrambled out, a scream came from Disco. "Wait, stop. It's Shannon, she's hurt."

Caine pushed everyone aside as he made his way back into the minibus. Once reaching Captain Thompson, he was shocked to see her pinned to the van where one of the spears had gone through the top of her leg. Captain Thompson was looking pale and barely conscious and just as he was about to make her comfortable gunshots were fired and there was a cry from Slick: "Smoggie old chap, if you would like to get yer groove on it would be quite fantastic as we have incoming."

Caine looked at Captain Thompson and apologized and threw a punch which knocked her out before pulling her leg and ripping it from the foreign object which had her pinned. "Come on Smoggie boy its getting rather busy out here," Slick screamed as everyone had grabbed a weapon and were struggling to hold the attackers back.

Caine crawled out of the van with Captain Thompson over his shoulder and made his way backwards towards Marske Road which would take him in the direction of the cliffs. The others stayed back slightly to give Disco, Caine and Captain Thompson a head start. Making their way down Marske Road as more and more Grendlar emerged from gardens and alleys, and while dragons and other creatures fell from the skies, destroying houses on their way to earth, it was getting to look very unlikely that they would achieve their objective. "Quickly, the station," Caine screamed as he made his way towards the small railway station in the heart of Saltburn. Once reaching the station, Caine put Captain Thompson onto the floor and attended to her wound as the others gave cover, including Disco. Even if his eyes were welded tight shut.

Once Caine had finished tending to Captain Thompson's injuries, he picked her up and made his way with Disco, surrounded by the others, the short distance to the beach, but once travelling the short distance up Milton Street on to Marine Parade it became apparent that they were not going to make it as more and more of the enemy's forces approached from every direction. They were overpowered and seconds away from being torn to bits when from the sky came Barack and Old O'Shea with dozens of their armies, at extreme speeds and ferocity. With these mighty beasts fighting back the hordes and taking damage shielding our young hero from harm, this gave Tyra and two of her griffon followers time to break through and fly the gang back to safety through a barrage of attacks trying to stop them reaching the safety of Mother Nature's realm.

CHAPTER XX

COURAGE AND TRADITION
WILL GET US THROUGH!

Tyra and her subjects flew Disco and the others straight into the centre of Mother Nature's courtyard and the gang dismounted and made their way towards Captain Thompson who was still unconscious. Suddenly Mother Nature came crashing through the great doors to the palace. Making her way straight for Disco with her arms held wide, she wanted to wrap them around our young hero but stopped at the last moment as she remembered the shard. Looking around, she suddenly stood up very business-like and a little embarrassed. Standing straight and looking down at Disco, Mother Nature informed him, "Danby my child, you do not know how pleased I am to see that you are safe."

Spotting Captain Thompson, Mother Nature made her way directly to her with a worried look on her face which seemed to turn to confusion for a split-second before summoning Fargle and having him take her for medical attention. Disco had been trying to pull at her gown the whole time but found it impossible as her gown was made from the purest life giving water.

"Mother Nature, Mother Nature, where's Mack? Please? Is he OK? Mother Nature?"

Mother Nature looked at Disco with half a smile on her face and told him that Mack was OK and that he would be along very shortly. Disco looked confused but overjoyed at the same time.

"But how? I thought I felt him pass away. I was sure. Please?"

Mother Nature said, changing the conversation and gesturing for them to make their way inside, "There is food and drink inside and we have a lot to discuss."

Disco was not quite sure what was going on but he was ecstatic that his friend had been brought back from the dead.

The five of them followed Mother Nature into the great hall and all but Disco were amazed at this wondrous room which was like nothing they had ever seen. Looking upon them as a proud mother would look at her child experiencing the world for the first time, Mother Nature just smiled and asked them to sit and eat. The table was laid out with a feast second to no other and the gang sat to eat. The main doors opened and in walked Fargle, to the amusement of the three soldiers.

"Mr. Danby sir. It is good to see you are OK," Fargle told Disco with a nod and a wink on his way to Mother Nature.

Mother Nature bent down to talk to Fargle as he whispered into her ear. As he turned and left the room Mother Nature informed them, "Your friend will be alright. She is still unconscious as she has lost a lot of blood. Please eat. She could not be in better hands."

At that Tackschmee ran in and made his way directly to Disco with his little arms held out. Disco scooped him up excitedly before pausing and looking Mack up and down. "Is it really you? I thought I had felt you pass away."

Tack pretended to be Mack immaculately as the Schmee share a consciousness, which meant that Tack could draw from all of Mack's memories; but with a burning pain in his heart for the loss of his brother, Tack did what he had to do. Disco was so pleased to see his friend safe and sound.

Spitting food from his mouth Ondre stated, "Sorry 'bout that." And wiping his mouth with his sleeve, continued, "Why can't the little fella and his boys do what they did at them holiday homes? Disco said there is thousands of 'em. Send 'em out and job's done."

Mother Nature looked confused. "Disco?"

"That's my new nickname," Disco informed her.

So with a lost look upon her face, Mother Nature continued, "The form that the Schmee took that day is a form that they cannot control. This dark creature is imprinted into the Schmee's DNA and can only be reached through deep, deep anger or fear. The truth is that when the Schmee left to collect Mack, I feared as much for your safety as I did for your attackers. So I am sorry, this is not an option."

"Well what's the plan?" asked Caine.

"For now you must rest. I have much to organize and we will speak in the morning," replied Mother Nature.

Caine flew up and shouted, "It seems that we have done nothing but lay around and in the meantime people are losing their lives out there. Now – what happens now? "

Mother Nature walked towards Caine and from the other side of the table from him, she explained calmly, "These realms are probably the best place to be at this moment as time travels much slower out there. I have trusted companions looking for answers. Once we have those answers we can start to join the dots. Until this time I am sorry but you will have to be patient. Now Fargle will show you to your rooms and if there is anything you need, please do not hesitate to ask." At that, Fargle entered the hall and gestured that the four of them should follow him.

Once through the door, they were met by the most beautiful pearlescent corridor that was reflecting a brilliant and warming glow. There were four huge doors in this corridor, two on each side. Each door was an entrance to the individual's ideal room. Dre had a room that showed his personality: enormous in size, with a highly polished oak floor and the rest of it looking like a typical Barbadian room, except for a white piano that was reflecting the light beautifully in the corner by an open fire and an oversized couch that you probably would struggle to escape from. It was the same for the others. Caine's room was a gamer's paradise, while Slick's was more refined and old English. Disco was the last to enter his room and was amazed but pleased to see his bedroom back at his great-grandmother's. Holding the replacement Mack, Disco ran to his bed and dived straight on it. Taking a moment to study Mack, he just accepted the lie as he was just so relieved to see his friend alive and well again.

The gang all ended up in Caine's room playing video games and listening to the Stranglers through his state of the art music centre. Whilst the others were playing, Caine sneaked out of the room to look for Captain Thompson. On entering the great hall, he was greeted by a very tired and ill-looking Mother Nature, sat there with her head in her hands and elbows balanced on the magnificent table. Caine walked towards her. Sensing his approach Mother Nature sat up and asked him, "Is everything alright? Do you need anything?"

"Yes and no. Thank you," Caine replied. "But it looks like you're not in such good fettle. Are you OK? You don't look good."

Mother Nature simply smiled. "I am alright, I promise you. Just tired from what is happening. Anyway, what can I do for you?"

Caine did not quite believe her but carried on to explain, "I was just looking for Captain Thompson. She must be awake by now?"

"You like her, do you not?" Mother Nature asked Caine who just blushed. "I am sorry but she has been returned to her family. She wanted to say goodbye, but as you know timing is of the essence in these uncertain times. I am sorry but she is quite safe and in good hands." Caine just put his hands in his pockets whilst staring at the floor and nodded gently, before turning and returning to his room.

The next morning the gang woke in their own time and after showering and finding their clothes washed and pressed, made their way to the great hall to have breakfast. Dre was the last to emerge from his room and on entering the great hall, was mystified to see it filled with gods and creatures from myth and legend.

"Ah, you finally decided to get up then idle lad? Come on we've been waitin on yer?"

Dumbfounded and misty-eyed, Dre made his way to his seat as the others sat there laughing at him.

"I am glad you are well rested my friend, as we have difficult times ahead," Mother Nature told him. "Now we are all together I think it is time to begin. Merlin is making his way to the meeting place of god, man and the fallen. You, I think, know it as Stonehenge. Here on this ancient and sacred plot our battle must come to a conclusion. Hard times are ahead of us my friends, but the end will play itself out soon enough.

They sat around the table all day and went through what was to happen with gods and legendary creatures and this made them feel pretty confident about the impending future. The gang spent the next few weeks in Mother Nature's realm, exploring and investigating as a lot of preparation was in the mortal realm and time was passing much slower for our heroes.

Pan once again was furious at finding out Disco was definitely still alive and at how they could lose him with what felt like unlimited resources being thrown at the problem. He had spent hours venting his frustrations and with crashes and explosions coming from Durnap's great hall, everybody thought it would be more prudent to stay on the other side of the door. Suddenly the doors flew open and Pan came crashing through, all sweaty and looking like he had been in battle for hours.

"Obviously I can trust no one to do my bidding as I ask, so I will do it myself. Send out scouts and find me that wretched boy. He will be with Mother Nature. Find me her plans," he screamed at his fellow gods before returning to the room with the great doors slamming behind him.

The day of reckoning had arrived and the gang got ready for their journey. None of them knew what was going to greet them, never mind how many times they had gone over it. Disco had already been there and took the morning reassuring them: "Don't worry. I keep telling you all, all we have to do is get through a mass of the enemy's creatures and make it to Stonehenge where Merlin will be waiting for us with an ancient shield to cover us. Easy-peasy."

The rest of the gang were not looking quite as confident as our young twelve-year-old hero. Mother Nature and our five heroes set off, accompanied by the gods Cernunnus and Herne, Mack and four of his brothers which were linked to Slick, Caine, Dre and Danby Senior, who were all desperate to give it a go, and the might of Old O'Shea and Barack the mighty dragon kings. Heading through a dingy and damp tunnel, the group reached the end after a mere fifteen minutes and came out into a beautiful meadow surrounded by dozens of tunnel entrances, like a giant airport with terminals all around. Cernunnus and Herne ran straight into the meadow and ran around like children.

"Are they OK?" Slick asked Mother Nature with a concerned look on his face, before looking to the others which had confused looks on their faces also.

"Do not worry," Mother Nature replied. "There are no better hunters or trackers in any other realm and I do not see the problem with taking time to celebrate beauty. Especially in these darkest of times."

Mother Nature stepped into the meadow and lifted her arms as she turned to face the others and like a scene from *Snow White*, birds and animals approached her with no fear or doubt at all. The others gave thought to what she had said and with the magnificent sight which was going on in front of them, they quickly started to understand.

Suddenly, Dre spun round with a very confused look fixed firmly too his face. "Did anybody else hear those two dragons speak?" he asked when a blustering reply came from Old O'Shea in a broad Irish accent, "You impudent, puny mortal," and sprinting to within inches of Dre's face, continued, "Your arrogance amazes me. You think you are the only race that has the intelligence to speak. It is that ignorance which landed you in this trouble in the first place."

Dre took a massive gulp and simply said "OK" and Old O'Shea walked off in the direction of one of tunnel entrances with Barack following, who looked to be sniggering. The others set off following before pausing to see a large black woman walking alongside them. Dre ran towards her –

"Mother?" – and the others were bemused, not as much as Dre though.

Mother Nature walked over laughing. "It is not your mother I am afraid. It is Ashschmee. It is very unusual for a Schmee to take a human guise but a combination of fear and the degree you must have wished for her to be here, somehow caused this."

The others started laughing and set off patting him on the back and calling him mammy's boy. Dre just stood there, looking his mother up and down in amazement before spurting out, "I don' like it! How do I change it?"

Mother Nature told him "Concentrate on a creature you want Ashschmee to become and it will be."

Dre started thinking and Ash started to wiz about like deflating balloon before in front of him stood Gyp, a large blue deerhound-cross-lurcher dog. Looking at Mother Nature, Dre informed her, "Now that's much better," before setting off to catch up the others and patting his leg for Gyp to come see him.

Following Barack and Old O'Shea into the giant entrance to one of the tunnels, the gang were amazed to find themselves perched on a cliff overlooking a deadly looking land with volcanoes and rivers of lava flowing through them. Mother Nature climbed on the back of Old O'Shea and with Barack following with Herne and Cernunnus on his back, they took flight.

"What the hell do we do?" asked Danby Senior.

Dre concentrated on the sleekest, coolest dragon he could whilst Disco being an old hand at this, went for the more comfortable ride of Pegasus the flying horse. "Just think," Disco shouted as he disappeared into the distance.

Caine and Danby Senior both started concentrating on the fastest dragon they could too and in seconds they stood before them. Jumping on their backs like excited children, the pair took off and flew as fast as possible to catch the others up. Dre spotted this and put his foot down. The three of them raced through volcanoes and canyons whilst yelling like kids at a funfair. After a couple of hours, Disco and the gods reached the exit which was only a few hundred metres from Stonehenge. They waited for nearly ten minutes for the 'children' to catch up and when they got there, their rides looked exhausted.

Looking at the three exhausted dragons, Mother Nature shook her head and simply said, "Do not worry my friends you may rest soon."

"Nice one. I'm shattered," said Caine.

"I was not talking to you," Mother Nature stated.

After setting down at the exit, Cernunnus and Herne jumped to the floor and made their way outside to do some reconnaissance before the others exited this realm. About three hours had passed in the realm and the three soldiers were getting impatient. "Something's wrong. We have to go look see what's gannin' on out there," said Caine.

Mother Nature stopped him and informed him, "Do not worry. It may seem like hours in here but it has only been a short time in your homeland. Please my son, learn to be patient."

It was about another seven hours before the pair re-entered the realm, and with bad news. "What kept you?" asked Caine before they got a chance to speak. Herne looked at him and informed him that they had only been gone for about five minutes.

"Look, back to business," interrupted Cernunnus. "Pan is out there in person. His forces are a hundred thick. It does not look good." Looking over to Barack and Old O'Shea, he added, "Oh well. Are you ready?"

At that, the pair gave out a deafening roar and turned to Mother Nature to inform her, "It is done."

"Now we wait," said Mother Nature to Caine, at which he thought this would be a great time to sulk. Mother Nature smiled at him. As she closed her eyes and raised her arms, suddenly a tree which had the sweetest and juiciest fruit hanging from it, but like nothing ever before seen by our heroes just grew from the clifftop floor on which they were perched and developed from seedling to fully matured in a matter of seconds and in front of their eyes. "Forgive me. You must need nourishment. The Jerra fruit will take care of all your needs."

The four mortals nearly picked the bountiful tree bare as they had never tasted anything so delicious in all the years that they had lived. It had been about twenty-eight hours since the mighty roar and our heroes took to exploring and anything else they could do to stem the boredom. Disco even introduced them to the game of cross morph which they found to be hysterically amusing, but the wait was long.

At last, the time was near to exit the realm and make their dash to Stonehenge. Slick had won the race earlier, so it was decided that his dragon would be used as the vehicle of choice and while the three gods mounted Barack and Old O'Shea the four mortals imagined the dragon that had beaten them for speed earlier on this adventure. Slick was grinning ear to ear as they flew back into the realm so that they would have a good run up to gather speed for their speedy exit to the mortal realm. They started to gather speed for their exit. Hitting the exit at these speeds was not as easy as once thought, as the convergence of the two timelines made them feel somewhat drunk. Disorientated, they flew about for a couple of minutes before coming round and realizing the magnitude of the battle going on all around.

The mighty roar of the two magnificent beasts Barack and Old O'Shea was to call together all there forces and for them to make way to this one spot to open a path for Disco and the others. Looking over to Stonehenge it looked magnificent, put back to its original glory and surrounded by a brilliant blue light like a laser show in a smokey room. Merlin had opened this shield and was eagerly awaiting Disco and his companions to join him. This was not going to be as easy as they hoped, as the enemy was aiming all their attentions on stopping them from reaching Merlin and the safety of the shield.

Pan was sat high above the clouds on Barrook, the most powerful and ferocious of all the Death Breathers. Spotting Disco making a run for the shield, Pan gave Barrook the instruction to attack. Flying ever closer to our young hero at incredible speeds, Pan's face was screwing up with an unholy rage which grew with every inch closer he got towards Danby. Just as Pan and Barrook reached Disco, Old O'Shea and Barack appeared as if from nowhere and a savage battle between the three of them ensued, but luckily this gave Disco just enough time to reach the shield, crashing to the floor and very nearly coming out of the other side. Disco had had the wind knocked out of him but returned to his feet as soon as he possibly could. Running to Merlin and out of breath still, Disco asked what he must do.

"We must wait for your father, child. From this spot with the combined force of two of Zeus's descendants and the shard present we hope to raise an army of the honourably fallen and scatter them across all lands to rid the Earth of the bamboo."

At that Danby Senior came crashing into the shield on Morraschmee.

"Quickly," Merlin instructed them "To the altar in the centre. Now face each other on opposing sides and with your hands on the altar, repeat after me." And Merlin spoke the words to awaken the fallen.

Once finished both Disco and his father looked at Merlin and asked, "What's supposed to happen?"

Merlin was stood there puzzled. "But it should have worked. Why did it not work?" Merlin placed the book on the altar and flicked through it violently, looking for some kind of answer. Stopping dead, Merlin looked at Danby Senior and asked, "Just where did you get this shard? Was it handed down to you?"

"Yes it was handed down to me. About four years ago by the wife's grandmother," Danby senior replied.

Merlin danced about in a rage screaming, "It is useless. Absolutely useless. Can nobody do anything correctly?" And stopping himself, he turned to Disco, bottling his rage and explained, "Your father Danby is not a descendant of Zeus like you. We need another member of your family from your mother's side and we have very little time."

"Uncle Caine, me mam's brother," Disco screamed.

"Yes, but we need them here now," Merlin explained.

"I know that," said Disco "But that's him outside fighting with the others. " And pointing outside, Disco showed him.

"We need him in here now," screamed Merlin.

Disco turned to Mack and Morra and told them to fetch his uncle Caine. Making their way outside the safety of the shield the two Schmee returned to the battle and tried their hardest to herd Caine towards Merlin and Disco who were waiting nervously. This was difficult though, as Caine did not know what was going on and thought he was doing the right thing by remaining in the battle and buying his nephew time.

"Someone's going to have to go out there," Danby Senior exclaimed before running from the shield and trying to attract Caine's attention. From out of nowhere a giant wolf landed on Danby Senior and pinned him to the floor. With eyes burning with the fires of hell and its breath with the stench of rotten and decayed meat, the mighty beast stood slavering only inches from Danby Senior's face and the colour had left him as he lay there motionless, as suddenly the beast threw its head back to strike.

Seeing this, Caine raced in the direction of the wolf and flew towards it as fast as he could before Danby Senior was done for. Caine arrived just in the nick of time and, crashing into this mighty beast, was thrown from his ride. Getting back to his feet, dazed and bruised, he made his way towards the brilliant blue light of the shield and the protection it gave. On entering the shield, he made his way towards the safety of Merlin's shield and arrived just in time to see Disco escape Merlin's grasp and return outside for his father. Grabbing his father by the scruff of the neck Disco dragged him until he had regained his wits enough to move under his own power. Dragons, griffons, birds and an array of other creatures threw themselves in the way of their attacking foe.

Finally Disco made it back to safety and as he got his breath back, Merlin flew towards him and grabbing him by the scruff of the neck he threw him towards the altar.

"Whoa a minute," Caine screamed but Merlin showed him no heed.

"Quickly, we must continue. I do not know how much longer I can power this shield."

Caine made his way towards the altar to take his place with Disco and Merlin immediately began again: "Antiquus nationis exsisto pepulli pravus de is ea id terra." (Ancient people arise and banish evil from this Earth.) The pair repeated this until the altar began to vibrate and spirits of ancient gods and royalty erupted from the centre like an erupting volcano and knocking everyone inside the shield from their feet. Making a barrier outside the shield and bringing an end to the fighting, the spirits stood tall and firm. A beautiful lady on a chariot approached Disco with 2 beautiful maidens, one on each shoulder and asked his name.

"Danby Dorello your majesty," he replied.

The figure smiled at him and flew off at high speeds with the rest following to make dust of the bamboo with a power supplied by the Earth itself. The spirits spaced themselves evenly across the planet like an array of satellites, with the lady on the chariot with her maidens returning and positioning herself high above the altar.

"Who is she?" Danby asked Merlin.

"That my child is one of my first mortal friends… That my child is her majesty Queen Boadicea and her 2 daughters. Three of the most beautiful and honourable people it has been my pleasure to meet." Merlin gave his reply with a warm and respectful look upon his face.

Suddenly a magnificent green light shot from the altar and straight into the air towards Queen Boadicea and dispersed through her and her daughters to the other gods placed in strategic points around the planet. This beautiful green light engulfed the planet and once the Earth was totally surrounded the light began to pulse and with every pulse the light got brighter and brighter.

No one there could imagine the impact this bright green light was having on the planet but Mother Nature and a large minority of the gods could feel it like a boa constrictor releasing its grip ever so gradually and allowing them to breathe freely once again. People from every village, town and city across the globe were emerging from their prisons in which the bamboo held them and singing and dancing radiated a good feeling across the globe. For this one brief moment people everywhere forgot their problems and feuds. All of a sudden things in their old lives seemed to be trivial and unimportant. Colour, nationality or religion did not matter for this brief moment of rejoicing and time of celebration.

Back at Stonehenge Disco was amazed by what was going on and asked Merlin what the beautiful green light was. "The beautiful light you are being lucky enough to witness is Gaia. Tied to Mother Nature, a great energy and consciousness flows through the Earth beneath your feet and is, as we speak repairing itself through those loyal to the planet and pure of heart and fed through Saint Michael's Ley line."

No sooner had these words left Merlin's mouth and Disco spotted Pan with a rage on his face and summoning a massive ball of energy in his hands as he was making a beeline towards Mother Nature. Disco ran and shouted as loud as he could, but to no avail as the light was making too much noise for him to be heard and Pan had already released the deadly ball. Mother Nature at this time was in sync with Gaia and was oblivious to the mighty energy ball flying towards her. Just as it struck, Disco jumped into its path and was thrown through the battle-weary for a good hundred feet. Suddenly a flash of light from nowhere sent Pan crashing to the ground and pinned him there. No one knew who was responsible but most of them were more concerned for Disco

As everybody ran to Disco, Mother Nature was still oblivious to what was going on and remained so for a further five minutes or so at which she fell to her knees with exhaustion. With the spirits returning, Queen Boadicea spotted the lifeless Disco and made her way towards him. Upon reaching Disco on her chariot, Queen Boadicea held out her hand and the spirit of Disco started to stand up to take it.

"NO, NO. DANBY PLEASE? NO, DON'T GO!" Danby Senior, Caine, Slick and Dre were screaming, "Please no."

Mother Nature at this time had managed to collect her thoughts and was making her way to see what was happening.

Starting to pick up her pace Mother Nature was devastated to see Disco stepping onto the chariot to make his way to the next world.

"Mother Nature, can you do nothing please?" Danby senior and the others pleaded with her.

Mother Nature just stood there motionless and in shock and replied in a quiet and broken voice, "I cannot...It is not in my power."

As Queen Boadicea and the chariot disembarked a massive explosion of bright light appeared in front of them and there in all his glory stood Zeus himself. Looking at Queen Boadicea, Zeus asked, "Please your majesty. If you could just bear with me for one moment and delay your departure for just one minute?"

Queen Boadicea nodded her head in agreement and immediately Zeus turned in Pan's direction with his face full of rage and made his way towards him. Looking down at Pan who was still pinned to the floor by the energy bolt, which we now know was sent by Zeus.

"YOU DARE TO STRIKE OUT AT A FELLOW GOD?" Zeus bellowed before making Pan disappear in an explosion of light similar to the one Zeus had arrived in. Making his way back towards Disco and the Queen, Zeus stopped and made an announcement: "THIS WAR IS OVER!" He screamed in a frightening bellow, "Tonight, god has attacked god. THIS IS THE END!" Zeus left it at that and continued in the direction of our life-impaired hero. On reaching Disco Zeus told him, "You are a brave young man with a pure heart. I feel that what has happened to you is my fault and I am reminded of the innocence of youth. Please, lay back in your body; and Queen Boadicea, I am sorry but it is not this young man's time."

As Disco went to exit the chariot Queen Boadicea stopped him and planted a kiss firmly on his cheek. Disco jumped off the chariot and with that Queen Boadicea returned to her eternal rest. Disco lay back down inside his limp, lifeless body as Zeus kneeled down on one knee and taking his right hand and placing it firmly on Disco's chest and raising his left arm to the heavens and clenching a tight fist, Zeus summoned a red lightning bolt which flew through Zeus's body and into Disco, making his lifeless corpse convulse. Zeus stood up and looked down on Disco as he opened his eyes in amazement and his father scooped him straight into his arms with a look of disbelief and relief on his face. The others all cheered and danced around in jubilation at this and putting Disco down, Danby Senior took him by his helmet and looked him straight in the eye and told him, "I love you so much son and am so very, very proud of you!"

Disco cuddled his father as hard as he could before turning to Mother Nature and running to take her in his arms. Flinging his arms around her, Disco noticed her flinch and immediately pushed away from her.

"I'm sorry, I'm sorry!" Disco shouted and started to remove his father's helmet for the first time in over two years. Removing the helmet revealed a massive afro of Ginger hair that just seemed to keep growing as it decompressed. Passing the helmet to his father, Disco got back to the job at hand, giving Mother Nature as hard a hug as he possibly could.

With everybody celebrating and congratulating each other, Danby Senior turned to Zeus to thank him but was amazed to see that he was nowhere to be seen. Merlin came over to congratulate Danby and thank him for his bravery before making his leave back to Lingfeln as there was still much left to do there. Everyone said their goodbyes and Disco thanked Old O'Shea once again and Barack for saving his and companions' lives. Mother Nature travelled home with Danby and the others over the mortal realm and felt a warm feeling watching the news spread that Britain and the rest of the world were now safe and watching the British people celebrate at this news. On reaching Saltburn, Disco and Mother Nature who were on the back of the great Pegasus and the others who had been racing Dragons again, landed on the beach and dismounted. The three sleek and slender dragons returned to their original form as Schmee and after cuddling their pairings, made their way back slowly towards the cliffs.

"We'll see you at home, kidda," Caine told Disco before ushering the others off the beach to give his nephew time to say his goodbyes.

Disco looked sadly into Mother Nature's eyes and asked her, "Is this goodbye then?"

"It looks like it," Mother Nature replied.

"I won't see you again, will I?" Disco asked her, but was relieved by her reply.

"I am a very busy being I must admit, but I think I could make time for the young man that saved mankind." Disco wrapped his arms around her once again and hugged her for all he was worth. "Come now. Your mother must be frantic. You must go to her, but remember what happened here Danby and spread the word. Things must change or one day there will be no Earth to protect. Every year I get weaker yet I put my faith in your race. Prove me right Danby? Please…? Prove me right." Mother Nature then stepped back onto Mack's back as Disco hugged his neck and told him he would see him soon.

As Mother Nature flew back to the cliffs to re-enter her realm, she picked the three Schmee up and disappeared into the cliffs in a flash of light. Disco turned round and headed for home but slowly as he was feeling much better about life and was quite enjoying the feel of the wind and rain, running through his hair.